BILLY BAKER'S DOG
WON'T STAY BURIED

Other Avon Camelot Books in the
SPINETINGLER *Series*
by M. T. Coffin

(#1) THE SUBSTITUTE CREATURE

Coming Soon

(#3) MY TEACHER'S A BUG
(#4) WHERE HAVE ALL THE PARENTS GONE?

SPINETINGLERS

#2

BILLY BAKER'S DOG WON'T STAY BURIED

M. T. COFFIN

AN AVON CAMELOT BOOK

BILLY BAKER'S DOG WON'T STAY BURIED is an original publication of Avon Books. This work has never before appeared in book form.

AVON BOOKS
A division of
The Hearst Corporation
1350 Avenue of the Americas
New York, New York 10019

Copyright © 1995 by George Edward Stanley
My Teacher's a Bug excerpt copyright © 1995 by Robert Hawks
Published by arrangement with the author
Library of Congress Catalog Card Number: 94-96282
ISBN: 0-380-77742-8
RL: 4.9

First Avon Camelot Printing: April 1995

CAMELOT TRADEMARK REG. U.S. PAT. OFF. AND IN OTHER COUNTRIES, MARCA REGISTRADA, HECHO EN U.S.A.

Printed in the U.S.A.

OPM 10 9 8 7 6 5 4 3 2

There was no turning back now, I knew. This was it.

I took a deep breath, stomped the thick black mud off my boots, and opened the front door to the Cape Flattery Veterinary Clinic.

I stood for a minute, just inside the entrance, dripping puddles onto the linoleum floor and remembering another stormy Christmas Eve, three years ago, right after we had moved to Cape Flattery, when Mom had given me Howard as a puppy. It was our first Christmas without Dad.

"Dr. Holmes?" I tried to keep my voice steady.

"I'm in the operating room, Billy."

I followed the voice down the dimly lit hallway and found the operating room at the end.

Inside, Dr. Holmes was standing beside a

large metal table. Howard was lying on top of it, held down by long leather straps. "I waited for you, Billy, but I was hoping you wouldn't come. I don't really think it's a good idea for you to be here when I put Howard to sleep."

"I have to. I promised Howard I'd stay with him."

Dr. Holmes shrugged. "I'm really sorry, Billy, but it's either this or a lawsuit against your mother, and you know she couldn't afford that."

"Please hurry."

I knew Dr. Holmes was only trying to make me feel better about the whole thing, but I wasn't quite sure how much longer I could stand being there.

I locked eyes with the dark brown pools that belonged to my dog. I wasn't quite sure whether I was seeing disbelief or betrayal or if dogs even knew about those things.

Then Howard's eyelids started to lower.

Above us, the fluorescent lights suddenly flickered.

Dr. Holmes looked up. "I hope they don't go out. We'll be in the dark for sure, without any windows in here."

A loud crash of thunder shook the room.

"What the—" Dr. Holmes said.

The flickering lights had now become

strobes, and everything in the room seemed out of focus.

Another crash of thunder forced me to grab hold of the operating table.

"I hate these winter storms," Dr. Holmes muttered.

Then the flickering stopped. The lights seemed to grow brighter.

Howard's eyes opened wide, and the brown pools were deeper than I had ever seen them before.

They began to draw me into them. I could hardly breathe. I felt as though I were drowning. I held on to the side of the metal operating table even tighter.

The lights began to flicker again, this time even more wildly, and thunder literally caused the room to tremble.

Then Howard closed his eyes completely, and the lights went out.

I held my breath.

"What was that all about?" Dr. Holmes finally said.

"He'll be back," I whispered. "Howard's coming back from the dead!"

2

The lights in the operating room buzzed back on.

Dr. Holmes was looking at me with a puzzled expression. "What'd you say?"

I turned away and looked down at Howard's lifeless body. "Nothing."

"Well, for a second there, I thought you'd been talking to that crazy Leonora Winter and the rest of those loonies at the Church of the Kingdom of Resurrected Pets." He shook his head in disgust.

I looked up, surprised. I hadn't even thought about that until now. "No. It was nothing." I was lying, of course. I really had seen *something* in Howard's eyes at the very moment of his death that had caused me to blurt out that he was coming back from the dead. But what

4

did it mean? Before, I had always thought things like that only happened in books and movies and on television, not in real life. Now, I wasn't sure. "I wish I hadn't come. I wish I hadn't seen this."

Dr. Holmes took a deep breath and let it out slowly. "I told your mother it was a bad idea, Billy, but she said you really wanted to be here, so I agreed to it. Of course, when I was your age, I probably would have done the same thing, too, if Howard had been my dog."

I wasn't comforted.

"Listen, Billy, I've made arrangements to bury Howard in the Cape Flattery Pet Cemetery. I hope that's all right."

I blinked from surprise. We couldn't bury Howard there. It cost money to do that. "We can't afford it, Dr. Holmes."

"I've taken care of everything, Billy. All you need to do is show up. In fact, one of the men from over there will be by shortly to pick up Howard and get him ready, and we'll have a really nice service for him around two o'clock this afternoon."

I didn't know what to say. Why would Dr. Holmes want to do this? I wondered. He'd been nice enough to Howard when he was alive, but he hadn't particularly liked him, I knew. Why

5

would he want to give him a funeral now that he was dead?

The only thing I could figure out was that he and Mom had gone to high school together, and they still seemed to be good friends. After we had moved to Cape Flattery, she had even worked for him part-time at the clinic, but then all of a sudden, she had quit. She never would tell me why.

Maybe Dr. Holmes was doing it as a favor to her, because Mom knew how much it would mean to me. I sighed. "Okay, then. Thanks."

I looked back down at Howard, and tears began to well up in my eyes. "I have to go now."

Dr. Holmes stopped me. He put an arm around my shoulders. "I know this Christmas won't be the same without Howard, Billy, but you will get over it, and, who knows, you might even find another dog in your stocking. I get a lot of requests here at the clinic to place dogs in homes, especially around this time of the year."

"I don't want another dog." I could hardly choke back the tears now. "I wanted Howard."

Dr. Holmes took his arm away. "Billy, you know this would have happened sooner or later, anyway, don't you?"

I looked up at him.

"I know Howard loved you, but he hated almost everyone else. He tolerated your mother, but when you weren't around, she was afraid of him. She told me so many times. Even when I'd try to treat him here at the clinic, he'd—"

"You just didn't understand him, Dr. Holmes," I interrupted. "*Nobody* understood him!"

Dr. Holmes shook his head. "Billy, animals are just like people in many ways. There are the normal types and the criminal types. You hear about human beings who commit horrible crimes, and you wonder what happened to make them do such terrible things. Well, it's my opinion that nothing happened to them. I just think this criminal behavior was there inside them all the time, and something set it off."

"You think Howard was a *criminal?*" What was Dr. Holmes trying to tell me?

Dr. Holmes put both hands on my shoulders. "You have to believe this, Billy. Howard was basically a bad dog, and I think if we hadn't put him to sleep, he would have eventually done something really awful to your neighbor, Mr. Calhoun, and maybe even to other people, too, including your mother."

I wanted to throw something at Dr. Holmes, I was so angry at him now, but I just didn't

7

have the energy. Anyway, I was sure what was making me feel that way was, deep down inside, I knew he was probably right.

I had never really wanted to admit it to myself or, for that matter, anyone else, but there had been a lot of times when Howard just didn't act like other dogs. It had finally all come to a head, when Howard bit our next-door neighbor, Mr. Calhoun, who had to be taken to the hospital to have his face stitched up.

On the other hand, I knew it had all been Mr. Calhoun's fault, too, so why did everyone blame Howard? For some reason, Mr. Calhoun was always taunting him. He kept at it until Howard did what any other dog would do. When he had had enough of Mr. Calhoun's taunts, he let him know it. That's all it was.

I had tried to explain that to everyone, including the police when they questioned me about what happened. I even told them about the time in the fourth grade when I punched George Wilson. He had been taunting me for weeks. When I had finally had enough, I let him have it, but nobody talked about putting me to sleep, so what was the big deal about Mr. Calhoun? Frankly, I thought he looked better after Howard rearranged his face!

I swallowed the lump in my throat. "Thanks

for doing all of this. I appreciate it, and I know Howard would, too." I turned and started walking out of the operating room. "I'll see you this afternoon at the pet cemetery."

"Wait, Billy. I can take you home."

"No, I want to walk." Besides, I was planning to take the long way home, and I didn't want him to know about it.

"This storm's really bad. All that thunder and lightning and cold rain. You'll get sick and miss the rest of Christmas."

That wouldn't mean a whole lot at our house, I thought. "I just want to be alone, Dr. Holmes. I've got a lot of stuff to think about." I also had something I needed to do. Dr. Holmes had given me an idea.

"Okay." Dr. Holmes looked at me. "I know you don't believe this, Billy, but I really do understand how you're feeling right now, and I can assure you that things will get better. It'll just take time."

More than anything else, I wanted to believe what he was saying, but Dr. Holmes hadn't seen what I had seen in Howard's eyes. I knew things would never be the same again.

The rain wasn't as heavy as it had been when I first got to the clinic, but the wind was stronger and it slammed an icy fist into my face when I opened the front door.

I crossed the street in front of the clinic and in just a couple of minutes had gone down the embankment on the other side, sliding in the mud.

Soon, I was hidden among the huge hemlock trees that lined Wolf Creek. I stopped for a minute and leaned up against one of them, letting the icy rain drops fall off the branches onto my face.

I had been wondering for weeks how I'd feel after Howard was dead, and it wasn't anything like I had thought it would be.

I didn't feel sad or angry or alone or any of those things. I just felt puzzled. What had I really seen in Howard's eyes as he was dying, anyway? It had been a message of some kind, I was sure, and when I had blurted out that Howard was coming back from the dead, I thought I had read the message correctly. Could I have been imagining it? Could this whole thing with Howard and Mr. Calhoun have just made me crazy?

Still, that was the only thing that had come into my mind at the time—and the message had been so strong! There had to be something to it. But how would Howard do it? I wondered.

How would he come back from the dead? And when? And why?

Well, there's really only one way you can find out for sure, I thought. I started walking again.

Wolf Creek ran through a large field of idle land that now all belonged to the Church of the Kingdom of Resurrected Pets. I could see the huge main building in the distance. I'd heard kids talking about the church ever since we'd moved to Cape Flattery. The only thing I knew about it, though, was that it was a place I was supposed to stay away from. It made Mom angry every time it was even mentioned in her presence. I think it had something to do with Grandmother Wallace's having given the church a lot of money before she died.

I stood looking at it, trying to get up the nerve to carry out the plans I'd made in Dr. Holmes's clinic. Leonora Winter was the minister of the church. She had a daughter, Hannah, who was in my class at school, although I'd never talked to her before. She was kind of weird, and kept mostly to herself.

What I wanted to do was go right up to the church building, knock on the front door, and ask Mrs. Winter if she could explain to me what I had seen in Howard's eyes, but the longer I stood there, with the wind blowing the cold rain in my face, the harder it became to walk inside. After about fifteen minutes, I finally decided to forget the whole thing. I'd just have to find out the answer some other way.

I started back across the field. I had to walk about two miles before I reached the next street.

I climbed up the embankment to a parking lot of a bank. From there, it was only five blocks to my house, but I'd have to pass by Mr. Calhoun's house before I got to mine.

From a block away, I could see Mr. Calhoun in his front yard. He had on his yellow rain slicker. His face was still half-covered with bandages. I had the feeling he was only wearing the bandages for show.

He's waiting for me, I thought. He's going to ask me about Howard. Well, let him, I decided. I'll never speak to him again in my whole life.

I even thought once about going around the block—so I could come to my house from the opposite direction—just to avoid Mr. Calhoun, but I quickly ruled that out. I wasn't going to let Mr. Calhoun intimidate me. I was just going to ignore him.

"Well, is he dead?" Mr. Calhoun's voice was dripping with hate.

I kept my eyes straight ahead. I wasn't even

going to look at this man who had forced me to have my dog put to sleep.

"I'm going to the funeral this afternoon! I just called Dr. Holmes, and he told me it was at the pet cemetery at two o'clock. I'm going to the funeral to make sure he's dead!"

I turned onto our front walk. I wanted to run up the steps, but I wasn't going to give Mr. Calhoun the satisfaction of knowing that my insides were being ripped apart and that I was about to burst into tears. No way! I thought.

Mom was sitting at the breakfast table when I came inside.

"You're soaking wet, Billy."

"I know."

"I could have driven you to the clinic, but you were already gone when I got up. I didn't know you had to be there so early."

"Don't worry about it, Mom. I'm all right. Anyway, I felt like walking."

"I just thought you might want to have someone with you, that's all." She sighed. "Oh, Billy, I'm so sorry this had to happen."

"I know you are, Mom."

She looked at me. "I heard shouting outside just now. What was that all about?"

I shook my head. "Nothing." All I wanted

now was to be alone. "I'm going to take a hot shower." I turned and headed toward my room.

"I'll have your breakfast ready for you when you get through. You need to eat something."

I whirled around. "Please, Mom! I'm not hungry! Okay? I just watched my dog die. I'm not hungry!" I stood looking at her for a few seconds.

There was absolute silence in the room, except for the drops of rainwater I was dripping all over the linoleum. "Howard's funeral is at two o'clock," I finally managed to say.

"*Funeral?* We can't afford a funeral for Howard!"

"It's not going to cost us anything. Dr. Holmes is paying for it."

Mom got a funny look on her face. "Oh."

I left before she could say anything else.

When I got to my room, I decided to forget the shower. I took off all my clothes, collapsed onto my bed, and started crying.

Mom woke me at one-thirty. "You need to hurry, Billy."

I tried to get out of bed, but my body refused. All I wanted to do was lie there and sleep. I wished now that Dr. Holmes had just taken Howard's body and done with it whatever vet-

14

erinarians do with dead animals when their owners can't afford to bury them in pet cemeteries.

At ten till two, I was finally dressed. As I started toward the front door, I suddenly remembered how Mom used to say you could always tell how important a person was by how many people attended his funeral. I wondered if that were true for dogs too.

Outside, the rain had stopped, but the wind was still fierce, and the cold knifed through me.

Mom was waiting for me in the car.

Just as I was getting into the front seat, I noticed Mr. Calhoun sitting in his car. He was looking our way. I knew he was probably waiting until we backed out of the driveway, so he could follow us. "He said he was going to the funeral, Mom, but I don't want him to be there."

Mom didn't say anything.

"I don't want him there, I said!"

Mom finally turned and looked at me. "Billy, if we try to keep him from attending, he'll probably cause us trouble again. He's that kind of a person. Just ignore him. We have to get all of this behind us. I can't take too much more."

I sighed. "Okay, Mom." My head was hurting

15

now. The cold wind wasn't helping matters, either.

For the most part, I had gotten used to living in northern California. Being this close to the ocean was fun and certainly a change from the dry climate of West Texas, but sometimes these cold winter storms made me wish we'd never moved.

Actually, we really hadn't had a choice. After Dad died, we lost our house and had to move into an apartment near the truck stop where Mom was working as a waitress. It was really awful.

Six months after that, Mom's mother, Grandmother Wallace, died, leaving us the house in Cape Flattery and a little money to live on. Moving to northern California just seemed like the right thing to do.

Now I wasn't so sure.

From time to time, I would turn around to see if Mr. Calhoun's car was behind us. It always was. I kept hoping he was just going to the grocery store or something like that, but every time we turned, Mr. Calhoun turned, too, and when we finally reached the pet cemetery, Mr. Calhoun was right behind us.

He followed us as we turned into the entrance.

16

At the far corner of the pet cemetery—which was actually larger than I had imagined—I could see Dr. Holmes and two other men dressed in overalls standing near an open grave.

Mom drove as close to the grave site as she could, then stopped the car.

"We'll have to walk from here," she said. "It's muddy, so be careful."

She tied a heavy scarf over her head, then the two of us got out of the car.

Behind me, I could hear Mr. Calhoun getting out of his car, too, but I refused to look at him.

When we reached the grave site, Mr. Calhoun was still behind us.

"Where's Howard?" I asked Dr. Holmes.

Dr. Holmes was looking at Mom, so it was several seconds before he answered me. "He's already in the shroud, Billy." He pointed down into the grave.

I moved closer to the edge.

There, at the bottom of the hole, was something that looked liked an old canvas bag. I couldn't believe that Howard was actually inside that dirty thing.

"I thought he'd be in a casket or something," I said.

Mr. Calhoun snorted.

17

I could see Dr. Holmes turning red with anger.

"This is the way we do it for animals," one of the men said.

I sighed. "I'm glad I didn't invite any other dogs, then. Howard would have been embarrassed." My voice cracked, so I didn't say anything else. I was absolutely not going to show Mr. Calhoun how upset I really was.

"Let's get started, then, Jim," Mom said to Dr. Holmes.

Dr. Holmes nodded. He said a few nice words about Howard, remembering some of the funny things he had done as a puppy.

I could see that Mom was crying. She had taken out a handkerchief and was wiping her eyes. I was sure it had nothing to do with what had happened to Howard, though. She had to be thinking about something else.

I turned away, so I couldn't see her, but that put me face to face with Mr. Calhoun, who now had a big grin on his face.

Dr. Holmes had finished speaking. "Do you want to say anything, Billy?" he asked.

I turned back around to face him. "Yes! I'm glad Howard chewed up Mr. Calhoun's ugly face! I just wish he'd done a better job!"

"Billy!" Mom cried.

"I mean it!" I could control my anger no longer. His smirk infuriated me and I wished I could punch him.

But Mom restrained me by grabbing hold of my arm. "Is that it?" she asked Dr. Holmes.

Dr. Holmes nodded.

"Wait! I want to shovel in the first spade of dirt," Mr. Calhoun said. He looked at me and smiled. "Just consider it another one of my Christmas presents, Billy."

"No!" I shouted.

But Mr. Calhoun had already grabbed one of the shovels off the ground and had done it before anyone could stop him. "Good riddance!" he said. Then he spat into the grave.

I broke free of Mom's grasp and lunged for him, but Dr. Holmes held me back with an arm around my neck.

Mr. Calhoun looked at me with blazing eyes. "Don't you dare lay a hand on me!" he shouted.

"He's coming back," I shouted back at him, "and when he does, this time he'll be the one who wins!"

3

Neither Mom nor I said a word to each other on the way home.

I just looked out the window at the swirling gray clouds. It would be raining again before long, I knew. I had learned to read the skies almost as well as people who had lived in Cape Flattery all their lives.

I wondered if the rainwater would soak far enough into Howard's grave to reach the canvas bag that Dr. Holmes had called a shroud. The thought of that made me shiver.

When we got back to our house, Mom finally turned to me. "What was all that nonsense about Howard coming back from the dead, Billy? It really seemed to upset Dr. Holmes."

"It wasn't anything, Mom. I was just mad at Mr. Calhoun, that's all."

"I know you are, Billy, but you can't lose control like you did back there at the cemetery. That's exactly what Mr. Calhoun wants. If you had attacked him, he'd have filed a lawsuit against us for sure, and that's the reason we had Howard put to sleep, so he wouldn't."

I opened my mouth, thinking maybe I should say something about what had happened that morning at the clinic, but Mom stopped me with, "I don't want to hear any more about this. It's over. Howard's dead. I'm sorry it had to happen this way, but it did, and there's nothing you can do about it now." Then she got out of the car.

I followed her into the house, went straight to my bedroom, and lay down again. I felt totally drained.

After a few minutes, I turned over and stared up at the ceiling. With the drapes drawn, the iridescent stars I had pasted onto them made me think of the many times I had lain out at night on the warm summer sidewalks, Howard at my side, looking up into the sky.

I sat up. I had to stop thinking about Howard. He was gone. I'd never see him again.

It was really stupid to think he was coming back. Dogs didn't come back from the dead. No one came back from the dead. I'd just have to . . .

No! I wouldn't stop thinking about it! I had to find out what Howard was trying to tell me before he died!

I stood up, left my room, and walked down the hallway to the telephone. I could hear Mom in the kitchen. She was busy making coffee.

That was fine. I didn't want her to know what I was saying on the telephone.

I looked up the number in the directory and dialed. After five rings, someone finally lifted the receiver, but whoever it was didn't say anything.

"Hello? This is Billy Baker. May I speak to Hannah Winter?"

"This is Hannah Winter."

The voice sent chills through me. "Oh, uh, well, I'm in your class at school, Hannah, and . . ."

"I know who you are."

I took a deep breath. "I need to talk to you right away. It's very important."

There was a pause. Then Hannah said, "I can be in the gazebo in the park in half an hour."

"That's great. Thanks."

I hung up the phone and went back to my room. For some reason, I couldn't stop shaking.

I spent the next fifteen minutes staring at a picture of Howard and me, trying to get up my courage again and wondering if I were doing the right thing by talking to Hannah Winter about what had happened. Finally, I stood up and left the room again.

"I'm going out," I announced to Mom.

"It's still raining, Billy."

"I haven't melted yet, Mom. Besides, there's someone I have to talk to." I started toward the kitchen door.

I thought she might try to stop me, but she didn't. She obviously had other things on her mind.

At first, I had hated the move to Cape Flattery, because it only had five thousand people in it, a real come down from Lubbock. But one of the things I could do here was go all over town by myself, and Mom never really minded. Actually, I usually did it with Howard. In fact, the park was one of our favorite places, so I knew where the gazebo was.

It was also in the park that I had first seen Hannah Winter, sitting alone, staring out into space, but I had never said anything to her before.

The only things I really knew about Hannah and her mother were what I had heard from the kids at school. They had come to Cape Flattery about five years ago, two years before

23

Mom and I had moved here. Mrs. Winter had started the Church of the Kingdom of Resurrected Pets in an empty building on Main Street.

At first the residents were angry, because of what they considered heresy and just plain bad taste, but then the money started to pour in, as people from all over the country arrived in Cape Flattery to become members.

So the people in town finally decided, after about a year, that it was a free country, and if the members of Mrs. Winter's church continued to behave themselves, well, they could stay. And so could all the money they were spending.

Hannah was sitting on the bench in the middle of the gazebo when I arrived at the park. Her bicycle was leaning up against the steps.

I waved.

Hannah didn't wave back.

That didn't stop me, though. I hurried over to the gazebo, shook the rain off my slicker, and sat down next to her.

"What did you want to talk to me about?" Hannah asked.

Suddenly, my mouth was all dry inside. "Well, uh, do you *really* believe that people's pets can, uh, come back from the dead?"

The expression on Hannah's face didn't

change, but she hesitated before she answered. "Yes. I believe what my mother preaches. Why?"

I swallowed and took a deep breath. "I think my dog Howard's coming back, that's why."

Hannah seemed to be studying my face. "What makes you think so?"

I told her the whole story, beginning with Howard's mauling of Mr. Calhoun, his threatened lawsuit, and finally Mr. Calhoun's solution to the problem. "I saw it in Howard's eyes, Hannah. I was there when Dr. Holmes put him to sleep. It was all so strange. The lights flickered on and off, and thunder shook the room."

"In case you haven't noticed, Billy Baker, we've been having storms all day."

I shook my head. "This was different."

Again, Hannah looked at me for several more seconds before she said anything. "My mother preaches that a Night of Resurrection is coming when all pets will come back from the dead and those of the true believers will be reunited with their loved ones. If you're a true believer, Billy, then you'll be able to participate in this glorious event."

"What do you mean, if I'm a true believer?"

Hannah smiled. "If you're a member of our church, Billy, then you're a true believer."

"Well, what'll happen to the pets of the people who aren't true believers?"

"They'll simply wander the earth in a state of perpetual limbo," Hannah replied.

That's a bunch of bunk, I thought, but I didn't see any percentage in saying so right then. "Well, when is this night going to be?"

Hannah shrugged. "I don't know *when,* Billy. No one knows when. My mother preaches that we should always be prepared for it, though." She stood up and looked me straight in the eyes. "Are you prepared?"

Her question had taken me by surprise. Before I could think of an answer, Hannah Winter had gotten on her bicycle and had ridden away without looking back.

I sat for several more minutes, wondering what I should do now.

When I finally made up my mind, I walked back to my house, hardly paying any attention to the cold rain.

Mom was sitting at the kitchen table, drinking a cup of coffee. "Are you feeling better?"

I nodded. "Yes." Actually, I was. I had made a decision. I really believed that Howard was coming back from the dead—whether I was a member of Mrs. Winter's church or not—and I planned to be ready for him when he did.

"Are you already in bed?" Mom asked, when she came into my room at ten-thirty, carrying a couple of Christmas presents.

"Yeah. I'm just really tired."

"I know. I am, too." She tried to smile. "Why don't you and I go ahead and open our Christmas presents?"

I wasn't in the mood, but I knew she was just trying to take my mind off Howard. I also remembered how much opening presents on Christmas Day upset her, now that Dad was dead. "Okay," I said. I got up and got Mom's present off the top shelf in my closet.

She gave me two flannel shirts, a pair of jeans, and some money.

I gave her a big bottle of perfume.

"This really smells nice, Billy." She looked at the bottle. "What's it called?"

I suddenly realized that I had forgotten to put a label on it. "Uh, well, it's called, uh, Alotta."

"*Alotta?* That sounds Italian."

"Yeah. That's it." Actually, I had mixed together *a lot of* perfumes I had bought at garage sales and put them all in one big bottle.

27

Mom set the bottle down on my bedside table. "Thanks."

"Thanks for the clothes and the money, too."

"Well, it really wasn't much of a Christmas for you. Things are just a little tight now. Maybe next year I can do better."

"Mom, these are great presents." I looked at her. "I wish I could earn some money to help out."

Mom sat down on the side of the bed. "Billy, if you're worried about whether we're going to have enough money to live on, then don't, because we still have some of your grandmother's money left." She smoothed back my hair, like she used to do when I was smaller. "It's all going to work out, okay?"

I wasn't quite sure I really believed her, but I said, "Okay."

Mom seemed to want to talk some more, but I yawned and closed my eyes for a minute, hoping she'd take the hint and go on to bed herself. I had plans. Hannah Winter and the other members of their church might not know when the Night of Resurrection would be, but I intended to be at the pet cemetery every night until it happened.

"I guess I'll go to bed, too," Mom finally said.

"Okay, Mom. Good night. Thanks again for

the presents." I hoped I hadn't said it too quickly to hurt her feelings or make her suspicious.

She kissed me. "Thank you, too, Billy." She stood up, picked up her bottle of perfume and left the room, closing the door on her way out.

At eleven forty-five, I opened my bedroom window, crawled out, and got my bicycle from the garage. For some reason, only nerds seemed to ride bicycles in Cape Flattery; most kids just walked. But I had brought my bicycle with me from Texas and rode it whenever I thought no one would see me . . . or when I didn't care whether they did or not.

The rain had finally stopped again, and the winds had died down considerably, but it was still bitterly cold.

By eleven-fifty, I was pedaling furiously down the street toward the pet cemetery.

When I reached the end of our block, I turned on my bicycle light. It wasn't very bright, but it did give me a yellow line to follow in the road.

When I reached the city limits, though, the light seemed to dim, and I realized then that I'd mostly been using the Christmas lights on all the houses to guide me.

Still, my bicycle light was bright enough to help me find the pet cemetery.

When I got to the main gate, I wasn't exactly sure what I was going to do, but I got off my bicycle and pushed it through the gate, which was closed but not locked.

I followed the graveled footpath until I saw the huge hemlock tree standing in the center of the cemetery.

Suddenly, I stopped.

I was sure something behind the tree had moved.

"Who's there?" I called out. My voice had a distinct quiver to it.

"It's me, Billy."

Hannah Winter stepped out from behind the tree. Actually, I could make out only a dark silhouette, but I recognized Hannah's voice.

I pushed my bicycle forward, listening to the crunching sound the wheels made on the gravel. "What are you doing here?" I whispered, when I reached the tree.

The light from my bicycle reflected in Hannah's eyes and seemed to make them glow. It was eerie. "I think tonight's the night we've all been waiting for, Billy, and I wanted to be here."

"I thought you said you didn't know when it would be."

"I didn't at first, but then I got to thinking about everything you had told me, and suddenly it all began to make sense. With all my heart, I now believe Howard's the one."

I looked at her. "The one *what,* Hannah?"

"You see, Billy, my mother preaches that there will be one special pet whose death will be a signal. The Night of Resurrection will be the first night after his death, and this special pet will rise from the grave and then lead all the other pets back with him."

I was stunned. "You think it's *Howard?*"

Hannah nodded.

"Well, if this is such an important event in your church, then why aren't your mother and the other members here?"

"I haven't said anything to them about it yet, that's why."

"Why not?"

"I wanted to be . . . well . . . positive."

"You could have at least called me. I might not have come out here tonight myself."

"It just never occurred to me to call you, Billy. I told you, if you're not a member of our church—even though Howard was your pet— you won't be allowed to participate in the reunification. It will be as though you simply don't exist. Howard won't even know you."

I just stared at her. That's what you think, I wanted to say, but I didn't. If Howard was coming back from the dead, no one was going to stop me from being there to welcome him. "Okay, forget it." I leaned my bicycle up against the tree next to Hannah's and turned off the light. "Have you been to Howard's grave yet?"

"No. I had just gotten here when I heard you coming."

I looked at the luminous dial on my wrist-watch. It was midnight. Christmas Day, I thought. "Well, let's go—"

Suddenly, I heard scratching noises coming from somewhere at the rear of cemetery. "Listen!" I whispered.

Hannah cocked her ear. "Is Howard's grave over there?"

I nodded. "Yes." I paused for a second. "Don't you think we should go find out what's happening?"

Hannah shook her head. "Even true believers aren't supposed to interfere with the resurrection, Billy. That's what my mother preaches. We should just stay here behind this tree and let it all happen as it's supposed to."

I breathed a sigh of relief. "Okay." Deep down, I really hadn't wanted to go just yet, anyway.

All of this was happening too fast for me. Just this morning I had watched my dog die, and now he could be coming back from the dead. It was almost more than my mind could handle.

From time to time, the fast moving storm clouds would break, letting the moon shine through, and making it easier for us to see.

But for the next fifteen minutes, nothing happened.

"You don't think it was just something trying to dig up Howard's grave to get at him, do you?" I whispered. The thought of some wild animal eating what was left of Howard was almost more than I could stand.

"No. It's not that," Hannah assured me. "I would have seen movement on top of the grave if it had been that. No, I'm sure the digging is coming from *inside* the grave. Howard's trying to get out."

We waited for several more minutes.

Finally, Hannah said, "He's out! I think I saw a leg!"

Then I saw something, too. It looked like two legs, in fact; although I realized my brain

33

might be creating these images for my eyes, because I wanted it to happen so much.

"His head's out now," Hannah whispered.

I watched, astonished, as Howard seemed to pull himself from his grave.

Finally, he was all the way out. He stood there for a minute, perfectly still, then he lifted his head and let out a howl that sent chills through me.

4

"He's never done that before," I said. I stood up. "I have to go to him. I have to see if he's all right." I started running across the cemetery toward where Howard was standing on top of his grave. "Howard! I'm coming!" I shouted. "Howard, I'm—"

Suddenly, Hannah grabbed me from behind and pulled me down. I landed with a thud on the cold, damp grass.

"You can't interfere with the resurrection, Billy!" she said. "I told you!"

I looked at her, rubbing my arm where I had landed on it. "Have you ever thought about trying out for the football team?"

Hannah gave me a dirty look.

"I have to go to him. He needs me."

"He doesn't need you. He won't even recognize you, Billy. You're not a true believer."

"He will. I know he will. Mom gave him to me when he was just a puppy. I was the only person he ever really cared about."

Hannah held onto my arm. "You'll see. That howling sound he just made? He's calling forth the other pets, so he can lead them back to be reunited with their loved ones. Wait and watch, as this glorious event unfolds. This is truly the Night of Resurrection, Billy."

Hannah was beginning to sound like one of those television preachers, but I knew I couldn't change the channel, so there was no sense in trying to argue with her now. "All right."

From where I had fallen, I could still see Howard through a field of tombstones, but for the first time, I realized that none of the graves were covered by marble slabs, like they were in a lot of human cemeteries. Here, there was only grass, and at the head of each grave was a white stone marker, with the name of the pet chiseled into it. I'd been so upset earlier in the day, at Howard's funeral, that I hadn't paid any attention to the rest of the pet cemetery. Now, with what seemed like hundreds of tombstones, it reminded me of those pictures I'd seen of military cemeteries.

For several minutes, I watched Howard

stand, unmoving, on the top of his grave, expecting to hear another chilling howl from him that would cause the other pets to rise from their graves, but instead he slowly began walking away.

Actually, Howard wasn't really walking. He was more or less lurching along. In fact, staggering might even have been a better description.

"That must have been some party."

Hannah looked over at me. "What?"

"Nothing." I had suddenly realized the tombstone we were crouched behind was next to the center footpath.

"If Howard keeps coming in this direction, Hannah, he'll walk right by us," I whispered. When she didn't say anything, I added, "This isn't what you said would happen."

"I know." It was said reluctantly, I could tell. "I don't understand it. I think Howard's planning to leave the cemetery without the other pets."

We continued to watch him. Howard was still walking slowly, but he wasn't lurching as much now.

All of a sudden, I wondered how I'd feel when Howard was right next to me. A few minutes before, what I had wanted more than anything

37

else in the world was to pick him up and hug him, like I had done when he was a puppy, but now I wasn't so sure. Hannah had been right. He wasn't acting like the same dog I knew. Maybe he really wouldn't recognize me after all.

I sniffed the air. "What's that awful smell?"

"It's Howard," Hannah whispered back. "That's the smell of the dead, Billy."

I shivered.

Then Howard was beside us.

For just a moment, I thought he'd pass by without stopping, but then he did.

He turned his head slowly and looked straight at me. Then he bared his teeth and growled slightly.

All of a sudden, I was terrified. This wasn't my dog. This was something else, something ... *evil*. I was wishing now that he hadn't come back.

Howard's hair looked all matted, too, and there were pieces of the shroud he had been buried in hanging off him.

I held my breath. What I really wanted to do was run from this dog I had loved for three years, but I couldn't move.

Finally, Howard turned away from us and continued walking down the footpath.

I let out the breath I had been holding. It sounded like air coming out of a punctured automobile tire.

"Are you all right?" Hannah whispered.

"I guess so." I looked at her. "You were right. He isn't the same dog that used to be my pet."

"No, I was wrong, Billy. I was so sure that Howard was that special pet my mother has been preaching about, but now, well, I don't know what to think."

"But he came back from the dead, Hannah! He was *resurrected*."

"Yes, but it's not happening the way my mother said it would. This is not what she preaches. Howard didn't call forth the other pets from their graves. Something's wrong."

I was really tempted to say, I told you so, but I didn't. Hannah seemed genuinely confused. Actually, so was I. "What are we going to do now?"

At first I thought she hadn't heard me, but then she finally said, "In a minute, we'll follow him to see where he's going."

I wasn't quite sure I wanted to do that, but I didn't say anything.

We waited until we thought Howard was far enough in front of us, that he wouldn't suspect what we were doing, in case it mattered to him, then we stood up.

"We need to hurry, or we're going to lose him," I said. Howard seemed to be walking faster now.

We ran toward our bikes.

Howard was already walking alongside the road when Hannah and I reached the gates of the cemetery.

We let him stay several yards ahead of us. We decided not to use our bicycle lights. The moon broke through the racing clouds often enough that we were able to keep Howard in sight.

When we finally reached the city limits, Howard trotted up onto a sidewalk and continued walking.

"He's headed in the direction of our house, Hannah. That means he must remember *something* about me, even if I'm not a member of your church."

Hannah didn't say anything.

"How am I going to explain this to Mom? What's she going to say when she wakes up in the morning and Howard's scratching on the back door, wanting to be fed?"

"I don't think you'll have to worry about that, Billy."

I looked at her. "What do you mean?"

Hannah stopped. "You're the first person I've ever admitted this to, Billy, but for as long as I can remember, I've always thought there had to be more to this than what my mother has been preaching all these years. I don't think that she or any other member of our church really understands why pets will one night come back from the dead."

I looked at her for a minute. "Do you?

"Yes, I think I do. At least part of it, that is."

"Well, why would *you* understand it, if your mother and the other members of the church don't?"

"I think about it all the time, that's why. The members of our church just accept what Mother tells them, and well, sometimes, Mother gets kind of carried away by all of this."

"If these pets aren't coming back for any glorious reunification with their former owners, Hannah, then why are they coming back?"

"They have important unfinished business to take care of."

"What do you mean? How can a pet have *unfinished business*?"

"I think Howard has something else in mind besides going back to your house."

I couldn't imagine what it could be, but I

41

didn't like the sound of Hannah's voice. "Really?"

She nodded. "Yes. Come on."

We started pedaling faster.

When we finally reached our street, Howard had already turned onto it.

"Look, Hannah! He's going straight to my house," I said. "I think you're wrong."

Hannah didn't say anything.

We continued to follow Howard on our bicycles.

Instead of stopping at my house, though, Howard walked past and paused in front of Mr. Calhoun's house.

I felt my heart stop. "Oh, no! I can't let him . . ."

Hannah held on to my arm. "You can't do anything about it now, Billy. This is the unfinished business I was talking about. If you've been mean to a pet in any way during its lifetime, then that pet will eventually come back from the dead to punish you. That's what I think this is all about."

I felt as though all of the blood had been drained from my body. "I didn't mean it, Hannah!"

Hannah gave me a puzzled look. "What are you talking about?"

I tried to pull loose from her grip. "I knew this was going to happen! I *predicted* it!"

Howard had already started up the walk toward Mr. Calhoun's front door.

"How could you have predicted this, Billy Baker? You have no say in what resurrected pets do! You're not a true believer!"

"It happened at Howard's funeral. I was angry that Mr. Calhoun was there. I told him Howard was coming back from the dead and when he did he was going to attack him again!"

Now, there was a stunned look on Hannah's face. She loosened her grip on my arm, and I wrenched free.

I began pedaling fast toward Mr. Calhoun's house.

When I was in front, I could see Howard at the door, scratching at it with one of his paws.

I got off my bicycle and let it fall onto the grass. "Howard! Please don't!"

On the second floor of Mr. Calhoun's house, a light came on.

"Howard, please come here. I'll take care of you." I knew I should run up and grab him, but some deep-seated fear kept me from doing it. "It'll be all right, I promise!"

Downstairs, another light came on.

Howard continued to paw at the front door.

"Howard! Don't!" I screamed at him, but a gust of icy wind suddenly hit me in the face, swirling the words around my head, and I was sure that Howard hadn't even heard me that time.

Then the front door opened.

Mr. Calhoun was standing there in his pajamas. The bandages that had covered most of his face earlier were gone. His mouth dropped open when he saw Howard.

He started to shut the door, but Howard gave a bloodcurdling howl and lunged at him. Mr. Calhoun ducked just in time.

I raced toward the front door.

When I reached it, Howard was already chasing Mr. Calhoun up the stairs. "Howard! Stop it!"

"Get this dog out of here!" Mr. Calhoun screamed. "He's supposed to be dead!"

Hannah was behind me now.

"Look what he's doing, Hannah! He's trying to attack Mr. Calhoun again!"

"He has to do what he came back to do, Billy!"

My head was swimming. Upstairs, I could hear Mr. Calhoun's terrified screams.

44

I raced for the stairs and began climbing them two at a time. "Howard, stop it. You can't attack him! I hate him, too, for what he did to you, but you can't attack him!"

Hannah had started up the stairs behind me.

When I got to the top of the landing, I saw Mr. Calhoun race through a bedroom door and slam it shut, just as Howard reached it.

"Get that dog out of here!" Mr. Calhoun kept screaming.

"Howard!" I walked slowly down the hallway toward him. Hannah followed.

Howard was now scratching frantically at the door, trying to get inside.

"This is really going to be difficult even for true believers to understand," Hannah said, "but we must all have faith, and we must trust our resurrected pets."

"What resurrected pets, Hannah? *One* dog, *my* dog, has come back from the dead to attack the person responsible for his death! How can you really believe this is some glorious Night of Resurrection? It's *evil*!"

Hannah looked at me with surprise. *"Evil?"*

"Yes!" I turned toward the bedroom door. "I've got to do something to stop him!"

"You don't have to do anything, Billy, so

45

don't worry about it. You're going to go home and wait until my mother decides what to do."

"Your *mother?*"

"Yes. She'll have the answer."

I just bet she will, I thought. "What about Howard, though? We can't just leave him here. He'll keep scratching until he gets in! When he finally does, he'll . . ."

Before I could finish, Howard suddenly stopped scratching and turned to look at us.

On the other side of the door, Mr. Calhoun was still screaming.

I took a deep breath and held it. I wasn't sure what was going to happen now. Maybe Howard was ready to do to us what he had tried to do to Mr. Calhoun.

It seemed like Howard and I looked at each other forever, but finally he turned away and began walking back down the hallway toward the stairs.

"Where's he going now?" I whispered to Hannah.

"I don't know. Everything's so different from what we all expected would happen on the Night of Resurrection, but I'm sure my mother will have an answer for this."

Keep talking, Hannah, I thought, and after a while you'll come up with a really good explanation for all of this. "I'm going to follow him," I said. I started toward the stairs.

Then Mr. Calhoun opened the door. "Is he gone?" he asked in a shaky voice.

"Yes," Hannah replied.

Mr. Calhoun looked at me. His face began to turn purple. "Then get out of my house!" he screamed.

"Gladly!" I shouted back at him. I started toward the stairs again. I didn't want to hear anything else Mr. Calhoun had to say.

Howard had already reached the front door by the time I got to the top of the landing. Then, for the first time, I noticed all of Mr. Calhoun's Christmas decorations. They were everywhere. In light of everything that had happened, though, they seemed totally out of place, but they gave me an idea. I turned and looked back at Mr. Calhoun. "He'll be back!" I shouted. "Just consider it my Christmas present to you!"

Mr. Calhoun slammed the door shut again.

Then I bounded down the stairs. I wanted to get away from this house and from Hannah Winter, too, but first I had to find out where Howard was going.

Unfortunately, Hannah was right behind me. I heard her close the front door.

She continued to follow me down the sidewalk.

I got on my bicycle. "You don't have to go with me. I'll take care of Howard myself."

"I want to help you, Billy. I need to understand what's happening here," Hannah said. "My mother will want me to . . ." She stopped. "Look!" She was pointing toward Howard.

I turned and looked. Howard had started to wobble and lurch again.

I pedaled over to him and laid my bicycle on the ground. "Howard?"

Howard looked up into my eyes. I could see the life going out of them. "Hannah, I think he's dying again!"

"He's not supposed to die again. He's supposed to be resurrected!" Hannah sounded almost hysterical. "I don't understand why it's happening this way." She was standing deadly still, staring at Howard.

"Maybe they're like, well, vampires or something, Hannah, and they can only come out at night."

"It's not supposed to happen like this!" she repeated.

I was sure she hadn't even heard what I'd said.

Then a plan hit me. It was so simple it was ridiculous. I was going to rebury Howard, and this nightmare would be over. I started toward him.

Howard didn't move.

When I touched him, it was all I could do to keep from jerking my hands away. His body was cold. His hair was stiff and wiry, something it had never been before, and there was still the odor that Hannah had called the smell of death about him.

I took a deep breath and closed my eyes. I put my arms around him and picked him up.

Then I carried him back to my bicycle. Hannah held it steady for me. With Howard under my left arm, I got back on and started pedaling toward the pet cemetery.

Hannah rode behind me, still not saying a word.

After only one block, I was sure I'd never make it, because Howard kept slipping as my legs went up and down on the pedals, but we finally got there. The eastern horizon had already begun to turn pink, something I hadn't seen in several days. It was still cold, but maybe the storms were over for a while, I thought.

49

Hannah held my bicycle for me again, while I got off. Howard lay still in my arms. Then she leaned both bicycles up against the gates and helped me carry Howard to his grave.

Using our hands, we dug away just enough dirt to allow us to put Howard back inside, then we covered him up and patted down the earth, so that it would look as though the grave had never been disturbed.

The fact that Howard was no longer inside the shroud didn't bother me this time, I was still so numb from what had happened. I was just glad that he was back inside his grave. Even after all of this, I still loved my dog and didn't want anything else bad to happen to him.

"Billy, do you think Mr. Calhoun will say anything about what happened tonight?"

"Not for a while, I don't. He's still too scared."

"Then you mustn't say anything about it, either, until I've talked to my mother." Tears were streaming down Hannah's face. "This could destroy our church."

I took a deep breath and let it out slowly. "Okay." I didn't really care anymore. I looked down at the muddy grave. "Good-bye, Howard,"

I said. Now, all I wanted was to remember how much I'd loved him when he was alive.

As we left the pet cemetery, tears were streaming down my face, so I didn't see the large cracks in the grass over the rest of the graves.

5

When I finally got home, it was already light.

I put my bicycle in the garage and climbed back through the window into my bedroom.

I took a quick shower, and then I got back into bed.

But my body wouldn't relax. I kept trying to make it, by doing all kinds of breathing exercises, but it wouldn't obey any of my commands. I guessed I was also hoping that, if I could just go back to sleep, when I awakened, this would all have been a bad dream.

It never happened. I just lay there, staring up at the ceiling, thinking.

Had Hannah already talked to her mother by now? I wondered. Had her mother decided what she was going to do? Actually, none of it mattered, anyway. Mr. Calhoun would sue us now for sure. We'd lose everything—again.

I realized I was slowly driving myself crazy. I just had to talk to someone. I couldn't wait until Hannah's mother told me what to do about it.

Mom would understand, I decided, if I explained everything carefully.

I got up, dressed, and went down the hall to the kitchen.

She had just started breakfast. She looked up when I came into the room. "Merry Christmas, Billy."

"Merry Christmas, Mom."

"Why are you always up so early? I don't think you've slept late once since Christmas vacation began."

I took a deep breath and let it out slowly. "I just don't want to waste my time, that's all. No other reason. I have a lot of things I want to get done."

Mom picked up a fork and turned over the pieces of bacon she was frying. "Still thinking about Howard?"

I nodded.

"Pancakes and bacon all right?"

"Yeah, that sounds good." I really didn't think I could eat anything, but I was going to try. I needed all the strength I could muster to tell her about last night.

When everything was finally ready, the two of us sat down at the table.

Rather than talking, though, which is what we usually did at breakfast, Mom picked up the morning newspaper and started reading the classified section.

She's looking for a job, I realized. She lied to me last night about Grandmother Wallace's money. It must be almost all gone.

All of a sudden, I knew Mom wouldn't understand. She'd already let me know she couldn't take much more of what was happening to us. With everything else that was going on, how could I now tell her that Howard had come back from the dead to attack Mr. Calhoun again?

I had to get out of the house. I had to do something to get my mind off this or I really was going to go crazy. Maybe I would just let Mrs. Winter take care of everything after all.

I stood up. "I'm not as hungry as I thought I was. Sorry, Mom."

She sighed.

I walked as deliberately as I could over to the kitchen sink, washed my hands, then started toward the door. "I'm going to ride downtown to see if Mr. Delacorte has any new comic books. I still need a few for my collection."

"It's Christmas Day, Billy. All the stores are closed."

"Not the comic book shop, Mom. Mr. Delacorte is always open on Christmas Day so kids can spend any money they got."

She shook her head. "Whatever happened to the time when . . ." She stopped and just stared into space.

I didn't want to hear the rest of what she was thinking. "I'll see you in a little while," I said. With that, I was out the door.

Just as I was getting my bicycle out of the garage, I looked over at Mr. Calhoun's house and saw him putting a couple of suitcases in his car. For some reason, I was surprised. He didn't seem like the type to run away, but I doubted if he'd ever come up against a living-dead dog, either.

Mr. Calhoun saw me looking at him, but he didn't say anything. I had to bite my tongue to keep from telling him that I thought he looked better with the bandages covering his face.

I watched him get into his car, start it, back out of the driveway, and head up the street. I didn't know what he was planning to do, but I was sure it included staying out of Cape Flattery for a while.

All of a sudden, I started feeling a little better. Could this nightmare be coming to an end? I wondered. Howard was back in his grave, and Mr. Calhoun was leaving town, so it looked like all of my problems had been solved.

Deep down, though, I really didn't think so. The solution just seemed too simple. After all, a pet—my pet—had actually come back from the dead, just as Mrs. Winter had been preaching all of these years. I doubted if she and the other members of the Church of the Kingdom of Resurrected Pets were going to forget that, even if Howard hadn't exactly done what Mrs. Winter had said he would. She'd probably just come up with a new version of what they were supposed to believe.

I got on my bicycle and started riding toward town. Today was one of those days I didn't care who saw me on it.

I was halfway down the street before I realized I didn't have my Christmas money with me, but I wasn't going back home to get it, I decided. I'd just look through the new comic books that had come in and have Mr. Delacorte put them behind the counter for me. I'd pay for them later. I often did that. Anyway, it was just something to get me out of the house, so it didn't really matter all that much.

When I got to the comic book store, a couple

of the guys from my class at school were already there.

The only one I really liked was Danny Crawford. He came over to me.

"I heard about your dog, Baker. Man, that was really mean of Mr. Calhoun."

"Yeah."

"You hadn't called me or anything. I thought maybe you and your mom went out of town for the holidays."

I shook my head. "No."

"How's it going?"

"All right. You?"

"My mom's making me do a lot of chores."

"Mine, too," I lied.

"Well, if you want to come over sometime during the break, give me a call, okay?"

"Okay."

I nodded at the other guy, Robert Fellows. He nodded back, but didn't say anything to me.

I started looking through the new comics.

Half an hour later, when Danny and Robert started to leave, Danny asked me if he could come over to my house that afternoon to see the comic book collection I was always talking about.

I put him off, saying Mom probably wouldn't want me to have any friends over on Christmas

Day, since it was a family holiday and we just sort of liked to share it together. I hated to lie to Danny, because he was the closest thing to a friend I had in Cape Flattery, but I wasn't in the mood for company. "I'll call you in a couple of days," I said.

"Well, okay, but don't forget!" he called over his shoulder.

"I won't."

When I had finally finished looking through all of the new comics and had asked Mr. Delacorte to put aside the ones I wanted to buy, I left the store.

I stood outside in the cold for a few minutes, wondering what I should do now. I didn't want to go back home. For a couple of minutes, I even thought about going to Hannah's house, to let her and her mother know that Mr. Calhoun had left town, but I decided against it. I just wasn't ready to talk to Mrs. Winter and find out what she was planning to do now that a pet had actually come back from the dead.

There was nowhere else to go, though, and I was beginning to get cold, so I got back on my bicycle and started home.

When I got there, a police car was parked in front. On the door, it said CHIEF OF POLICE. There was a policeman sitting inside. Mr. Calhoun must have called the police before he left town, I thought.

The policeman got out when he saw me. "Are you Billy Baker?"

I nodded.

He walked slowly up to me. "I'm Chief Rury. Are your parents home?"

"Mom's home. Dad's dead." I couldn't believe that had come out of my mouth. It was such a stupid thing to say.

But Chief Rury didn't seem to notice. "I need to talk to you and her right away. It's very important."

"Okay." I was trying to act as though I had no idea what it might be about, but I was sure I wasn't doing a very good job of it.

Chief Rury started up the sidewalk toward our front porch.

When I didn't follow him, he turned around and looked at me.

"I have to put my bike in the garage," I said. "Just a minute."

I could have leaned it up against the front porch steps, like I had done hundreds of times, but I needed to get away, if only for a few seconds, to think about what I was going to say.

I put the bicycle in the garage and went back

around to the front porch. Chief Rury was standing at the door.

I opened it and let him follow me inside. "Mom?"

Mom appeared from the kitchen. "What's the matter, Billy?"

"This is Chief of Police Rury. He wants to ask us some questions."

Mom looked puzzled. "What's wrong?"

Chief Rury looked around. "Could we sit down, please? This may take a few minutes."

"Oh, yes, of course. I'm sorry. In here." Mom led us into the living room.

Mom sat on the sofa. I sat in a chair to her left.

Chief Rury sat in a chair facing us. He picked something out of his left eye, looked at it, then flicked it out into the room. "About an hour ago, I got a telephone call from Mrs. Leonora Winter." He cleared his throat. "Mrs. Winter is the—"

"I know who Mrs. Winter is," Mom said, interrupting him.

Chief Rury cleared his throat again. "Yes, I guess most people in Cape Flattery do. Well, anyway, Mrs. Winter told me about an unfortunate incident that happened last night to your neighbor, Mr. Calhoun. She got the story from her daughter Hannah. Myself, I'd like to hear it directly from your son Billy."

So Mr. Calhoun hadn't called the police before he left town after all. But why would Mrs. Winter have called them? Was this her solution to the problem?

Mom was looking at me. *"Billy?"*

I shrugged my shoulders and gave her an "I don't know what he's talking about" look.

She turned back to Chief Rury. "I don't understand. Has something happened to Mr. Calhoun?"

"That's hard to say, Mrs. Baker. Mr. Calhoun has disappeared."

"Disappeared? Well, why would Billy know anything about it? We weren't exactly friendly neighbors, which I'm sure you already know."

Chief Rury turned to me for the answer.

"What happened to Mr. Calhoun?" I asked.

"You know what happened, Billy. You even predicted it, didn't you? That's why I'm here."

Mom stood up. "What's going on here? What does a police investigation have to do with the Church of the Kingdom of Resurrected Pets, anyway?" She was breathing heavily now.

That's what I was wondering, too.

Chief Rury continued to stare at me. I was beginning to break out in a cold sweat.

"Are you accusing my son of something? Are you planning to arrest him?" Mom screamed. "What? What?" She was getting hysterical.

Finally, Chief Rury said, "Please sit down, Mrs. Baker. No, I'm not here to arrest your son. In fact, I'm actually here to invite him to become a member of our church."

Mom went pale.

I couldn't believe what I was hearing. This guy wasn't playing with a full deck.

"Your son witnessed something last night that all of our church members would be very interested in hearing directly from him." Chief Rury smiled.

Our church members? Was Chief Rury a member of the Church of the Kingdom of Resurrected Pets, too? I was really beginning to get suspicious now. What was this guy up to? I wondered.

Mom was staring at him. "What are you talking about?"

"Have you ever attended any of our church services, Mrs. Baker?" he asked.

"Why in the world would I want to do that? I don't believe any of the nonsense that woman preaches."

I could feel my heart pounding, and I was starting to get short of breath.

"Maybe you should, Mrs. Baker," Chief Rury said. "Maybe you should."

It was suddenly so quiet in the house that I could hear the ticking of the clock on the wall.

"Do *you* believe what she preaches?" Mom finally asked him.

"Yes. Of course, I will admit that I was a doubter when I first started attending with my wife, after we had our darling Brownie put to sleep, but now . . ."

Mom looked at him. "What do you mean *now?*"

"It seems that Billy's dog Howard came back from the dead last night and tried to attack Mr. Calhoun again!" Chief Rury paused. "The problem here, Mrs. Baker, is that I don't believe Mrs. Winter fully understands what she's unleashed. I therefore feel it's my duty, as Chief of Police of Cape Flattery, to step in and take over. If I can bring Billy into the church, then we'd have a member whose pet has actually been resurrected. That would attract new members and new members mean more money for me, uh, I mean for the *church*."

So that's it! I thought.

Mom seemed to be having trouble breathing now herself. "How in the world could something like this happen?"

Chief Rury turned slowly back to me. "Billy, why don't you tell your mother here all about it? You were there. You knew it was going to happen." The tone of his voice was almost pleading.

"Billy was home in bed all night!" Mom screamed at him. "He doesn't know what you're talking about!"

They were both looking at me now.

I still refused to say anything.

"Come on, Billy. Tell us what happened." Chief Rury had a big smile on his face. "I need your help. Don't you see how important this is?" I suddenly had visions of him getting down on his knees. "What do you say, Billy?"

Without any more hesitation, I said, "I don't know what you're talking about."

Chief Rury knew I was lying, but I didn't care. Mrs. Winter could preach to people from now on if she wanted to about pets coming back from the dead to take care of unfinished business or whatever she had now decided they were coming back to do. Chief Rury and the other members of her church could believe her or not. As far as I was concerned, it was over. Even though Howard had attacked Mr. Calhoun a second time, what could they do? Kill him again?

I looked Chief Rury straight in the eye. "I don't know what you're talking about," I repeated. "I was at home in bed, asleep all night."

Chief Rury stood up angrily, knocking over his chair. "I can assure you of one thing, young man! You will become a member of the Church of the Kingdom of Resurrected Pets, whether you want to or not!"

Mom shot me a hard look to check if I was lying, I guess, then she stood up, too. "Don't you dare threaten my son like this. I just don't have any explanation for all of this, but if Billy says he doesn't know anything about it, then he doesn't know anything about it."

Chief Rury nodded at her. He didn't look at me again.

After he was gone, I got up and started toward my room, but Mom stopped me. "I want the truth, Billy. What was that all about?"

I turned and looked at her. "Nothing, Mom. It was about nothing at all."

"Well, you told me that . . . Well, you said something about Howard's coming back from the dead. You know you did."

"Oh, please, Mom! Do you believe that dogs can come back from the dead to attack people?"

"Of course not!"

"Then there's nothing to worry about, is there?" I turned and headed down the hallway.

I stayed inside my room for the rest of the day. I came out only when Mom called me to dinner.

At first, she didn't say anything, but she didn't have to. I could tell by the expression on her face that she had been thinking a lot about Chief Rury's visit.

She looked nervous, and she kept dropping things.

Finally, she said, "I want to know why Howard came back from the dead to attack Mr. Calhoun again."

I almost choked on the mashed potatoes I had in my mouth.

I started to lie again, but then I looked into her eyes, and I thought, I might as well get this over with. "To take care of unfinished business."

Mom gasped. "What do you mean, *unfinished business?*"

I swallowed hard. "When pets come back from the dead, Mom, they come back because they have things they need to take care of."

I couldn't believe I was actually even saying this. There was almost total silence, except for Mom's labored breathing.

Finally, she said calmly, "What *things,* for instance?"

"Well, if a person has been mean to a pet during its lifetime, then that pet will come eventually back from to dead to—to . . ."

"To *what,* Billy?"

"To attack him," I said, almost in a whisper.

Mom looked down at her plate and started eating again.

I did the same.

When I finished, I stood up and said, "I think I'll watch some television."

Mom didn't say anything. She just continued eating her food in silence.

I went into the living room and turned on the television set, but there were no programs that interested me.

So I stood up, turned off the set, and started toward my room.

Mom was washing dishes. I wanted to help her, but I didn't feel like it, and I thought she probably wanted to be alone, anyway.

I went to my room and got into bed.

I tossed and turned for about an hour, but I finally fell asleep.

During the night, I awakened with a start.

I looked at the bedside clock. It was 2 A.M.

Then I heard a scratching sound. It was

coming from the side window of my bedroom.

I listened to it for about five minutes, thinking it was just the branch of a bush being whipped back and forth by the wind, hoping it would eventually stop.

When it didn't, I got up, walked over to the side window, and looked out.

There, standing on his hind legs looking in, was Howard.

"Howard!" I cried.

Then I realized Mom might have heard me, so I whispered, "Stay right there!"

I dressed as quickly as I could. All kinds of horrible thoughts were racing through my mind. I couldn't imagine what Howard was planning to do now.

Since I didn't want to scare him away, I crept down the hall and out the back door. I had to go through a side gate to get to my bedroom window. When I finally got there, though, Howard was no longer standing under it. I looked around frantically, and then I saw him standing at the end of the driveway, watching me.

"Howard!" I called again.

There was no acknowledgment. He just turned and started walking away.

Does he want me to follow him? I had to

admit that I was still a little afraid of him. The Howard who had tried to attack Mr. Calhoun was not the Howard I had taken care of since he was a puppy.

I knew I had no choice, though. "Wait, Howard!" I called.

But Howard just ignored me and continued walking down the sidewalk.

In the distance, I thought I could hear a lot of barking and meowing. What's going on here? I wondered. I'd never heard anything like that before in Cape Flattery.

As had happened the night before, Howard was walking steadily now, but slowly, so it wasn't difficult for me to follow him. He'd probably come back to take care of Mr. Calhoun and discovered that he was gone, but what did he want now?

Then it hit me! Dr. Holmes had put Howard to sleep. Had Howard also come back to attack him? Did Howard want me to know of his plans? Well, if he was, he had a big surprise in store. There was no way I was going to let that happen!

Across the street, I saw two dogs and three cats walking in the opposite direction. Then one of the cats broke away from the others and turned up a sidewalk in front of a house.

That's odd, I thought. That cat looks like Mrs. Durant's cat, Peaches, but she's dead. She died sometime last year.

Up ahead Howard had turned a corner. We were now heading in the opposite direction from Dr. Holmes's clinic.

Something inside me told me that I should go back to Mrs. Durant's house, but I didn't. I continued following Howard, staying a few feet behind him. I had to see what he was up to.

We crossed two more streets.

When we reached a small red brick house, Howard finally stopped and stood looking toward the front door.

I stopped and looked, too. "Why did you bring me here, Howard?" I said to him.

Then I heard screaming coming from inside the house, and suddenly I knew why I was here. The Night of Resurrection had begun!

Howard growled and bared his teeth at me.

The screaming from inside the house continued.

I ran up onto the front porch and started knocking on the door. Over my shoulder, I could see that Howard still hadn't moved. Evidently, he wasn't going to stop me from trying to help whoever it was inside the house.

"Hey, let me in!" I shouted.

"Help me! Oh, help me, please!" a woman's voice screamed from inside. "Oh, please help me!"

I tried the door, but it was locked. I jumped off the front porch and looked inside a window. There was a light on at the back of the house. I couldn't see anything, but I could still hear the woman's desperate cries for help.

Above them, I thought I could also hear the high-pitched meows of a cat.

I ran around to the back door and tried it, but it was locked, too.

Finally, I found a side window through which I could see what was going on.

A large black cat had attached itself to an old woman's back. She was pawing at the cat, trying to get it off her, but the cat held firm. It was using one paw to scratch the woman's hand, when she tried to grab it.

Then the woman fell to the floor.

I looked around frantically and finally found a board leaning up against the fence. I sent it hurling through the window, breaking out the glass, so I could get in.

"Help me!" the woman cried. "Please help me!"

"Stop it!" I shouted to the cat. "Stop it!" When that didn't work, I yelled, "Here, kitty, kitty! Here, kitty, kitty!"

That didn't work, either. Actually, I've just never had much luck with cats.

I was finally able to hoist myself into the house through the window, but in the process I cut my hand on a small shard of glass that I hadn't seen. But I knew I couldn't worry about that now! I felt totally responsible for what was happening to this woman. I reached the cat, grabbed it around the stomach, and pulled it off the woman's back. The woman screamed and ran to the bathroom, locking the door behind her.

The cat was struggling so hard to get away from me, I had to drop it. It raced to the bathroom door and started scratching at it frantically.

What was I going to do now? I wondered.

Then I saw a walking cane in the corner of the room. I grabbed it and started to hit the cat across its back, but then I thought, Stupid, it's dead! You can't hurt it!

I had to find a telephone and call for help.

I looked around and finally saw one under a magazine on the table next to the bed.

I picked up the receiver and dialed 9ll. When a voice answered, I said, "A woman's being attacked by her cat!"

"What?"

"Listen, it's true! I don't know her name, but the house is on Elm Street and the telephone number is 555-2483. You've got to do something! The Night of Resurrection has begun!"

For several seconds, there was silence on the other end of the line, then the voice said, "I can only save Mrs. Foster if she joins the church, Billy. I'll be right there to sign you both up. Tell Mrs. Foster to have her checkbook ready. I'll collect from you later!"

I slammed down the receiver. Chief Rury! I couldn't believe it!

The cat continued to scratch at the bathroom door. I didn't want to leave the old woman alone, but I had to get out of there. I couldn't let Chief Rury find me.

I walked as close to the bathroom door as I could, managing to stay clear of the cat's paws. "Ma'am, if you can just hold on until dawn, you'll be all right!"

"I don't understand," the woman said in a shaky voice. "What do you mean?"

"I know this may be hard to believe, but your cat will die again at dawn and won't come back until tomorrow night. Stay where you are until the sun comes up!"

"Are you sure?" She still sounded terrified.

"Yes, I'm sure. Oh, and there's something else, too."

"What's that?"

"Don't let Chief Rury talk you into joining the Church of the Kingdom of Resurrected Pets!"

"What?"

"I don't have time to explain it now. Just take my word for it!"

I decided to leave by the front door, which I left open. I had no idea how the cat had gotten in, but I was going to make it easy for it to get out.

I stopped for just a minute outside to catch my breath. Howard was nowhere in sight. I had to be in the middle of a nightmare, I was sure, but I knew I wasn't going to wake up from this one.

I was responsible for everything that was happening, I knew. After all, it was my dog who had first come back from the dead to attack Mr. Calhoun, just as I had predicted. Had Howard now brought the other dead pets back with him to do the same thing?

"Help me! Help me!"

A girl was running down the sidewalk in front of the old woman's house. She was being chased by a large Doberman.

"Help me!" she screamed again.

The Doberman lunged at her, but the girl turned away just in time, and the Doberman plunged into a hedge.

"Kathy!" I shouted. I recognized her from my class at school.

Kathy stopped and looked around, trying to decide where my voice had come from.

"Over here! It's Billy Baker."

"Oh, Billy, help me!"

I ran toward her.

The Doberman was climbing out of the bush, but it seemed disoriented.

I grabbed Kathy by the arm and started running with her. "If we can make it to my house, maybe you'll be safe," I said. I actually didn't believe that for a minute. When Chief Rury found out that I wasn't at Mrs. Foster's house, my house would be the next place he'd look. None of us would be safe then. Now that the Night of Resurrection had begun, he'd really put the pressure on me to join the church, because it was my dog who was in charge of what was happening.

Behind us, I could hear the growls of the Doberman. It sent chills through me.

I was almost dragging Kathy along the sidewalk now.

"I can't go on, Billy. I have to stop and rest."

"We can't stop, Kathy. That dog'll attack you if we don't keep running."

"Oh, Billy, help me! I don't know what's happening."

Well, I certainly do! I thought. At least I thought I did, but I couldn't stop now to explain it to her.

We were almost to my house.

I knew the Doberman was picking up speed.

Finally, we crossed the street to my block.

"Just two more houses," I said.

Kathy began to collapse onto me. I didn't think I'd be able to carry her, but there wasn't anything else I could do. She was smaller than I was, so I stopped just long enough to throw her over my shoulder.

Behind us, the Doberman had also crossed the street.

For some reason, it seemed to be moving in slow motion, but I was sure that it was only because my eyes had begun to play tricks on me.

We were past the second house on the block now and had only a few more feet to go before we got to mine.

On my shoulder, Kathy was moaning.

I felt something sticky on the side of my face

and realized it had to be her blood. The Doberman had obviously already had its teeth in her.

We were in front of my house now.

I almost dragged Kathy up the front steps.

Idiot! I thought. The door will be locked. I suddenly remembered that I had gone out the back door!

The Doberman had already started up the front walk.

I dragged Kathy toward the side railing of the porch and pulled her over it, but I landed unbalanced, and we fell to the ground with a thud.

Kathy cried out in pain.

I picked her up, but I didn't have time to throw her over my shoulder again, because the Doberman was headed straight toward us. I began dragging her under my arm.

I dragged her through the side gate and then to the back porch.

I opened the door, dragged Kathy inside, and then locked it.

I set her down in a chair, and then I collapsed against the kitchen table.

At the door, the Doberman was scratching and growling ominously.

I wanted to turn on the light, but I was afraid to. I didn't want the Doberman to be able to see us. I wasn't sure what other ways these living-dead pets had of getting into houses. They weren't ghosts, I knew, because they had solid form, so they probably couldn't just come through the walls of the house, but then who knew what they were capable of doing? They might be able to get at us some other way.

The Doberman continued to scratch and claw at the door.

"Kathy! Wake up! You've got to tell me what happened!" I began shaking her. "Wake up."

Kathy moaned. Then she sat up and screamed!

"It's all right. The dog's outside. I don't think it can get in."

Suddenly, there was a loud howl and more pawing at the door.

"My dog wants to attack me, Billy, but how can it? It's been dead for three years! You've got to help me!" She dissolved into sobs.

"I'm not going to let it attack you. You'll be safe here." I didn't know whether I was lying or not, but I was going to try to keep my word.

"Who's in here?"

The light came on in the kitchen. Mom was standing at the door.

"Billy!" Mom cried. "What . . . who's that?"

79

"It's Kathy Wilson, Mom. She's in my class at school."

Mom came into the kitchen. "What's wrong with her? Is she . . ."

Before she could finish, the Doberman howled again and started clawing at the door.

"What's that?" Mom had started toward the door.

"Don't!" I screamed at her. The Doberman continued to claw at the door. "If you open it, that dog'll attack Kathy!"

Outside, I heard a car screech to a halt in front of our house.

Mom went to the window and pulled the curtain back. "Who could that be at this hour of the morning?"

"I'm sure it's Chief Rury!" I said. I looked at her. "We've got to get out of here!"

"No, Billy. Tell me it's not true."

"But it is, Mom, it is! Howard's come back from the dead again, and this time he's brought all the other pets in the cemetery with him!"

7

I ran to the front door, unlocked it, then said, "Come on!"

Mom gave me a puzzled look but helped me carry Kathy down the hallway toward my room without saying anything.

As we passed her bedroom, I said, "Get your car keys."

Mom hurried in and grabbed her purse.

Then we almost dragged Kathy the rest of the way.

Once we were inside my room, I locked the door. "When Chief Rury finds out the front door's unlocked, he'll let himself in, I'm sure. Then we'll climb out my window and go see Dr. Holmes. He'll know what to do."

"What if my dog hears us leaving?" Kathy said. Her voice was very weak.

"I'll latch the gate before we get into the car,"

I said. I just hoped the Doberman wouldn't be there waiting for me.

"Where are you, Billy?" Chief Rury called. He was inside the house.

"Now!" I whispered. I climbed out the window, ran to the side gate, and latched it as quietly as I could, then I helped Mom out the window. Together, we were able to pull Kathy through and get her into the back seat of our car.

"Billy, I think we really need to take her to the hospital," Mom whispered.

"Chief Rury'll probably go there first, Mom, especially if he sees any of Kathy's blood on the floor."

"Well, we have to do *something* for her. I think she's going into shock."

In the distance, I could hear Chief Rury calling us. It sounded like he was also beating on my bedroom door. Good, I thought. He still thinks we're inside.

"Dr. Holmes can take care of her, can't he?"

"He's a vet, Billy! He works with *animals!*"

"Well, he has medicine, doesn't he? Antibiotics are antibiotics aren't they?" I paused. "Dr. Holmes may also be in danger, Mom. He put Howard to sleep, and Howard may be planning to attack him, too."

"Oh, Billy, no!"

"I don't know that for sure, Mom, but we shouldn't take a chance."

Mom started the car and backed out of the garage.

Chief Rury didn't run out the front door, as we were leaving, so I was hoping he hadn't seen us. When he did finally realize we were gone, he wouldn't know in which direction to follow. That would buy us time.

On the way over to Dr. Holmes's house, I filled Mom in on everything that had happened since Howard had awakened me.

When we finally got there, we parked in front. It was all dark inside, but Mom noticed a light on in the back of the clinic, which was next door.

"He works too hard," Mom said. She wasn't talking to me, I knew.

I jumped out of the car and ran to the front door of the clinic. I knocked as hard as I could. It took several seconds, but Dr. Holmes finally answered.

"Billy! What the . . ." He stopped when he saw Mom getting out of the car. I knew then by his expression what I had suspected all along. He and Mom were more than good friends, and it gave me a funny feeling in my stomach. I still thought of Mom as being married to Dad, even though Dad was dead. But, I guess that explained why Mom didn't want to work at the clinic anymore.

"Jim, we need your help!"

Dr. Holmes hurried out to the car, picked up Kathy, and then all of us headed into the clinic.

At the door, Mom stopped. "I'd better drive the car around back so it won't be seen."

Dr. Holmes gave her a puzzled look but didn't say anything.

He immediately laid Kathy on the operating table—the same one that Howard had been put to death on—and started examining her. There was a wound on the back of her neck, which her long hair had been covering, but it didn't look too serious.

Dr. Holmes turned to me, just as Mom came into the operating room. "What happened, Billy?"

I looked over at Mom. "Tell him," she said.

So I did.

"You really expect me to believe that?" he said when I had finished.

I don't know what I had expected, but this wasn't it. "You have to, because it's all true! In fact, since you're the one who put Howard to sleep, he may be planning to attack you, too!"

Dr. Holmes turned to Mom.

She nodded. "It might not make any sense to you, Jim, but right now there are all these *living-dead* animals running loose in Cape Flattery!"

Dr. Holmes looked down at Kathy.

"Her Doberman was chasing her," I said. "He's been dead for three years."

"But this goes against everything in nature—" Dr. Holmes began saying.

"Is Kathy going to be all right?" Mom asked, interrupting him. I could tell she wasn't in the mood for any arguments. She seemed irritated that Dr. Holmes didn't believe us. She knew what was happening and at the moment didn't want to take the time to convince him.

Dr. Holmes sighed. "I've bandaged the wound, but we really should get her to the hospital."

"We can't," I said.

"Why not?"

"Because if Chief Rury finds her there he'll let the Doberman attack her again, unless she joins the Church of the Kingdom of Resurrected Pets, that's why!"

"That's preposterous!" Dr. Holmes said.

"It's true," Mom said. She told him about Chief Rury's visit earlier in the day and how he'd tried to get me to join the church. "I think he sees Billy as being essential to his plan to make a lot of money, since Howard is Billy's dog and Billy witnessed Howard's resurrection in the pet cemetery."

Dr. Holmes looked back at me. "Why do you think these pets have come back from the dead?"

"Well, I don't think it has anything to do with whether you're a member of Mrs. Winter's church or not. The only thing I can figure out is that they've come back for revenge. In Howard's case, Mr. Calhoun forced us to have him put to sleep." I looked down at Kathy. Her eyes were closed. She had evidently fallen asleep from exhaustion. "I guess she must have done something mean to her dog, too."

Dr. Holmes shook his head in disbelief. He sighed deeply. "Well, we can't just leave this girl here. I have a friend at the hospital. He can get her in and take care of her himself, and nobody will know about it. He won't even admit her. I just don't have what she needs here."

Dr. Holmes wanted Mom and me to stay at the clinic, but I didn't want to. No matter how much I had hated Mr. Calhoun, there was no way I could ever accept that any of this was supposed to happen to anyone else.

Mom agreed that we should go, too.

So Dr. Holmes brought his Jeep around front. We thought it would be less suspicious, because Chief Rury would probably be looking for our car.

I helped Dr. Holmes put Kathy in the back. Mom rested Kathy's head in her lap.

As we sped through the streets of Cape Flattery, we could see what looked like hundreds of dogs and cats roaming around.

"I've never seen so many of them in my whole life," Mom whispered. "It's horrible."

"Yeah, whoever thought people's pets would come back from the dead to attack them?" Dr. Holmes said. "It still doesn't make any sense."

"Nothing makes much sense, anymore," Mom said.

Actually, this all reminded me of a horror movie I had seen once, but I decided not to tell them that. All the people died at the end!

We finally arrived at the hospital. The place was lit up like daylight. There were cars everywhere, but none of them were police cars.

We parked in a secluded place at the back of the hospital. Dr. Holmes lifted Kathy into his arms. Mom led the way, and I brought up the rear.

We found a side door that was open and went in.

Hospital workers were running around frantically. No one paid any attention to us.

We found a room that looked like a lounge, and Dr. Holmes laid Kathy down on a couch. "You stay here with her," he said to Mom. "I'll go see if I can find my friend." He turned to me. "Billy, you go see if you can find out what's going on."

I left the room. Most of the people in the building seemed to be heading toward a room at the end of the hallway, so I followed them.

When I got there, people were standing around everywhere. Some of them had crude bandages all over their bodies.

"Give me your attention, please!" I turned and saw our family doctor, Dr. Jonah Durant, standing at the front of the room. "For some reason, there are all these vicious animals roaming loose in Cape Flattery. It's the weirdest thing I've ever seen! I've talked to the Chief of Police, but I'm not getting any cooperation from him. He keeps wanting me to join the Church of the Kingdom of Resurrected Pets! I've also tried to reach the State Police, but all the phone lines are down because of the storms. Do any of you know what's happening?"

I opened my mouth, but before I could say

anything, an elderly man in the back of the room stood up. "I can tell you what happened to me. My dog Pistol Pete woke me up scratching at my front door around two this morning, and he's been dead for ten years! He looked okay, but he sure did smell funny."

There was a murmur from the audience.

"Well, I opened the door for him, and he raced right into the bedroom and jumped on my wife's side of the bed. He seemed disappointed that she wasn't there. She's gone to visit her sister over in Winona."

"What'd he do then?" someone else asked.

The man shrugged. "He just went back out the door and didn't even look my way. I twisted my ankle running after him. I came here to get that taken care of and then I heard about all of this other stuff going on."

"Did your wife like your dog?" I asked the man.

"She hated him. In fact, I was surprised he came looking for her like that."

"I'm not," I said. "If she'd been there, your dog would have attacked her."

Everyone in the room stared at me.

"Billy, what do you know about all of this?" Dr. Durant asked me, but before I could reply, another doctor whispered something into his ear. Dr. Durant turned back to the audience. "People, this is even worse than we thought. Reports are coming in from all over town of people being *attacked* by cats and dogs and other animals!"

Another man stood up. "I tried to leave town, to take my wife to her doctor over in Wellston, but I had to bring her here instead. The police have blocked all the main roads. They're not letting anybody out of Cape Flattery. They told me we've been quarantined because of the attacks. They think we might have some rare disease."

"They can't make those kinds of decisions!" Dr. Durant shouted.

The man held up a flyer. "The police are also trying to get everyone they stop to join the Church of the Kingdom of Resurrected Pets. It costs a lot of money to do it, but it seems to be the only way we can be saved."

"I think I can explain everything, Dr. Durant," I said.

So for the third time that evening, I told everything that had happened, from the time Howard had died until our arrival at the hospital with Kathy.

Everyone listened in silence.

Finally, Pistol Pete's owner, said, "I know it

sounds crazy, but I have to believe this young man. Many's the time I caught my wife taking a switch to that dog, and he wasn't doing anything except being a dog, either."

Dr. Durant looked at me incredulously. "You knew your dog was going to come back from the dead, Billy, and you didn't tell anyone?"

"I did tell someone. I told Dr. Holmes, and I also told Mom."

"And they didn't do anything about it?"

"Would you have done something about it? They just thought I was upset about Howard's death and that it was something I wanted to happen."

"Well, what about when you actually saw your dog coming out of his grave? What about then? Why didn't you do something then?"

"It was all like a dream, Dr. Durant. I didn't know what to do?"

"Was it like a dream when you watched him try to attack Mr. Calhoun the second time?"

I was getting scared. The whole room seemed to be angry at me. "No."

"Well, what about afterward, Billy? Why didn't you let someone else know about it then?"

"I thought it was all over. I thought when we reburied Howard, that would be all of it."

"Do you believe you have to become a member of the Church of the Kingdom of Resurrected Pets to be safe?"

I shook my head. "No. I think they're coming back from the dead to attack people who were mean to them when they were alive. I don't think it makes any difference if you're a member of their church or not."

"Have any of the church members been attacked?" someone shouted from the back of the room.

I shook my head. "I don't know."

"Then maybe we should join!" someone else shouted.

"I'm not a member of the church," I said. "My dog started all of this, and he hasn't attacked me. He's had plenty of chances, too, so that's why I believe you don't have to be a member."

"You should have told someone else about all of this when it first started!" several people shouted angrily to me.

"Don't blame Billy for what happened!"

Everyone in the room turned and looked. Dr. Holmes was standing at the back next to Mom. "I should have listened to him. If anyone's to blame, then it's me."

The anger was now transferred to Dr. Holmes, but that didn't make me feel any better.

"Quiet!" Dr. Durant said. "No matter how angry we really are, we can't start blaming people now. We have to save lives." He turned back to me. "I'm sorry, Billy."

"That's okay."

"So you think they'll go back to their graves before morning?"

I nodded. "Yes. That's what I think Howard was doing after he attacked Mr. Calhoun, but I was afraid he wouldn't make it, so I carried him back myself, and Hannah Winter and I reburied him."

"Why do you think they go back, Billy?" Dr. Durant asked.

"I think they're sort of like vampires. They can only come out at night. They have to sleep during the day."

Dr. Holmes looked out the window, then he looked at his watch. "It'll be dawn in about an hour. I say we take some men and go to the pet cemetery and wait for them."

"What'll we do when we get there?" someone asked.

"We'll figure out something," another person said. He was brandishing a shotgun.

Several other people in the room held up guns, too.

I decided not to remind them that these pets

were already dead, so it wouldn't do any good to shoot them.

"Won't it be dangerous?" somebody asked.

I shook my head. "If they all act like Howard, then it won't, because toward dawn, Howard could hardly move."

That seemed to satisfy everyone.

So, with Dr. Holmes in the lead, we rode in a procession out of town and toward the pet cemetery. Since the road to the cemetery dead-ended there, we didn't expect the police to try to stop us. I was just hoping they wouldn't even know what we were doing. I really believed Chief Rury had decided if he could just keep all of the citizens of Cape Flattery from leaving town, the resurrected pets would scare them into joining the Church of the Kingdom of Resurrected Pets and make him a very rich man.

Along the way, I spotted some dogs and cats near hedges and corners of houses, but there didn't seem to be nearly as many as there had been earlier.

"Oh, Mom," I said, suddenly remembering, "how's Kathy?"

"She'll be fine. She's in good hands."

As we neared the cemetery, I wondered again what we were going to do once the pets returned.

Before we reached the gates, Dr. Holmes said, "We'll park along the side of the road here, and then we'll gather at the back of the cemetery and wait for them."

So that was what we did.

We waited until dawn.

We waited until a brilliant red ball began to peek over the eastern horizon and slowly light up the pet cemetery.

We could see that all of the graves were empty. They lay like gaping sores in the morning sun.

We waited until mid-morning, but none of the resurrected pets showed up.

"Where are they?" Dr. Holmes demanded. He looked at me.

"They must be sleeping all over town," I replied, "waiting until night comes, so they can start attacking people again."

95

Everyone started back toward town.

When we reached the city limits, we could see people staggering out of their houses. They all looked dazed. Most of them were still dressed in their pajamas and gowns.

As we drove further into town, we kept seeing more and more people on the sidewalks. Some were talking to each other. Others were carrying wounded people in their arms, stumbling around in circles.

"Stop!" I cried.

I had recognized Danny Crawford's father. He was carrying Danny.

When Dr. Holmes pulled the Jeep to the curb, I jumped out and ran over to them. "What happened, Mr. Crawford?"

Mr. Crawford looked at me and began shak-

96

ing his head. "Danny's gone into shock. Some cat attacked him!"

"What cat, Mr. Crawford?" I knew Danny had once owned a dog, but I didn't think he had ever had a cat as a pet. In fact, I was sure Danny hated cats.

"I'd never seen it before. It had an orange body with black feet."

I froze. I suddenly remembered hearing Danny talk about such a cat. It had come into their neighborhood a couple of years before and had given Danny's dog Bone all kinds of problems.

Bone lived in the Crawford's backyard and was supposed to be a guard dog, but Bone wasn't very bright. The cat must have realized it, Danny had theorized, because the cat ate Bone's food and in general made Bone's life miserable. Danny was almost embarrassed for Bone and tried several times to get his dog to defend his territory, but instead Bone just hid from the cat. Danny kept trying to find the cat's owner, but he never could.

Finally, out of frustration, Danny had lain in wait for the cat and had shot at it with a pellet gun. He had only intended to scare it off, and he thought it had worked. Later, however, he had found some blood and realized that he had probably wounded the cat, but he never found its body. Its owner must have found it, though, and buried it in the pet cemetery. Now it had come back for revenge.

Dr. Holmes had gotten out of the Jeep. "Do you need any help, Mr. Crawford?"

"I really do. My wife's in the house with dog bites all over her, too. She keeps telling me it was this old mutt I kept around for a couple of years, but he's been dead almost that long."

"You go take care of your wife, Mr. Crawford," Dr. Holmes said. "We'll take Danny to the hospital for you."

"I'd really appreciate that, Dr. Holmes," Mr. Crawford said. He looked at him with glazed eyes. "What's going on here, when a cat and a dog can attack your family like this? They never did anything to those animals."

I didn't know about Mrs. Crawford and the mutt, but I did know about Danny and the cat. It was precisely because Danny had done something to the cat that he had been attacked. I wished now I had told Danny what was going on when I had seen him at the comic book shop. Maybe he would have been more careful.

Mr. Crawford started back toward the front door of his house.

Dr. Holmes laid Danny in the back seat of

98

his Jeep, and I covered him with a blanket. Then we started toward the hospital.

Out of the corner of one eye, I could see that Mom was staring at Danny, probably thinking that it could just as well have been me. I didn't say anything to her, but I just wished we had taken her home, and that she hadn't come with us to the cemetery. I wasn't quite sure if she was going to survive all of this.

When we finally reached the hospital, there were people everywhere.

"I'll take Danny inside, Billy," Dr. Holmes said. "You stay here with your mother."

"He's my friend," I said. "I want to go with you." Then I realized how that sounded, and I looked over at Mom.

"I'll be all right," she said. "Go on."

Dr. Holmes opened the back door of the Jeep and lifted Danny out. I noticed I had some of his blood on my jeans, but I didn't care. I got out and began following Dr. Holmes into the hospital.

A man who passed us on the way said, "They don't have any more beds in there. They're putting the new ones on the floor." So much steam was coming out of his mouth, from the cold air, that it was like his head was in a cloud. All of a sudden, I started laughing.

Dr. Holmes looked at me. "Maybe you'd better stay outside, Billy."

I didn't argue.

I stood there, shivering, watching and listening to people as they came and went.

All of a sudden, I wondered where Howard was at this very moment. It occurred to me that he might be hiding somewhere around our own house.

When Howard was alive, he was always lying under some of the bushes in the backyard, even in the winter, where he could watch what was going on.

He had often reminded me of those nuclear missiles that were fired from submerged submarines, the ones that just exploded out of nowhere. That was what Howard used to do.

Dr. Holmes finally came out, and I walked back to the Jeep with him. "It's terrible in there."

He must have known I was having problems, because he put his arm around my shoulder. It felt really good.

When we got back into the Jeep, Dr. Holmes said, "I have to get you two out of Cape Flattery. You can't spend another night in this town."

I looked over at Mom. I could tell she was trying to decide what she should say.

"I'm going to take you back to your house so you can pack," Dr. Holmes continued. "I'll get some of my things together and be back by in about—"

"We can't just leave Jim," Mom said, interrupting him. She looked at me.

I turned away. Why did Dad have to die?

For what seemed like a very long time, no one said anything, then Dr. Holmes said, "I don't know where yet, but I do know that I want to take both of you with me wherever I go." He took Mom's hand in his.

I swallowed hard.

"Oh, Jim, I just need to think."

When we finally got to our house, Mom got out of the car without saying anything to Dr. Holmes.

I said, "It'll be all right. I'll talk to her."

"We can't wait too long, Billy. After tonight, it may be too late." Then he drove off.

Mom was curled up on the couch when I went inside. I sat down beside her. "I just don't understand why those crazy people are letting this happen."

"They believe they're right, Mom, that's why."

For several minutes, neither of us said anything, then I stood up and started out of the room.

"Where are you going, Billy?" Mom asked me.

"I'm going to Hannah Winter's house."

"What for?"

"I have to find a way to put an end to all of this."

"That's exactly what they want you to do, Billy. They'll make you join that church and then you'll be one of them!"

"I can't think of anything else to do, Mom." I left the room. Behind me, I could hear her sobbing.

I got my bicycle out of the garage and started pedaling in the direction of the Church of the Kingdom of Resurrected Pets.

All along the street, there were people with long sticks, beating the bushes around their houses, looking for the resurrected pets, I was sure. Everyone in Cape Flattery must have found out that during the day the pets had no life in them, that they were just existing until night when they could start attacking them again.

A patrol car crossed the intersection in front of me, and I had to brake. The policemen inside were using a loudspeaker to tell the people that the only way they could be saved was to join the Church of the Kingdom of Resurrected Pets.

Chief Rury was trying every approach, I realized.

Then I noticed one of the policemen looking my way.

"I'm already a member!" I shouted.

He smiled.

I began to pedal faster. I had to get out of there before they recognized me.

When I finally got to the church, I leaned my bicycle up against one of the porch pillars and rang the doorbell.

Hannah answered. She was wearing a heavy coat. She had a worried look on her face. "I was hoping you'd come."

I hesitated for just a minute.

When I finally entered the room, it felt even colder than it was outside, and that scared me.

Hannah looked at me. "It isn't always like this, Billy, only when my mother is communing with the dead."

I swallowed hard. "Is that what she's doing now?"

Hannah nodded. "Come this way."

I followed her up the stairs, down a long hallway, and into a room that wasn't too different from my own, except that the cold had penetrated even in here.

"Tell me all that's happened since I saw you last," Hannah said.

I told her.

She only nodded.

Suddenly, the temperature of the room seemed to rise, and I felt warm again.

Hannah stood up. "She's finished. She'll be here in a minute."

I stood up, too. I'd never met Hannah's mother, although I had seen her at a distance.

I noticed the knob on the door begin to open slowly and in a minute Mrs. Winter appeared, framed in the doorway. She looked frightened. "Why are you here?"

That question surprised me. I'm not quite sure what I had expected from her, but it wasn't that. "I just want all of this to end, Mrs. Winter. Can't you do something about it?"

Mrs. Winter shook her head. She came into the room. "It's out of my control, Billy. Your dog Howard's in charge now." Her voice was barely above a whisper.

"What's going to happen?" I asked.

"No one who has ever harmed a pet will be safe. The living-dead pets will sleep during the day and attack during the night. They will do this over and over and over until the end of time."

It was strange, but I believed every word she was saying.

Then I noticed Hannah staring at the doorway.

I turned and looked.

Chief Rury was standing there. "That's why we need you in our church, Billy," he said.

"No!" I cried. I raced out of the room, almost knocking Chief Rury down as I did.

I had absolutely no idea what I was going to do now, but I knew I had to find some other way to put an end to this nightmare besides talking to Mrs. Winter.

Hannah was right behind me. "Wait for me, Billy, please! I want to help!"

When I got to my front door, I stopped suddenly. The shades were all drawn. The house looked completely deserted. I was really scared now. I realized then that I should never have left Mom alone. I stood there on the sidewalk for several minutes, dreading having to go inside, wondering what I'd find.

"Billy!" Hannah called.

I turned. "What do you want?" I thought I had lost her.

She stepped out from behind one of the trees. "I want to help you!"

"Why?"

"I don't want anything to happen to you." Hannah hesitated for a minute. "I don't want anything to happen to anyone else in Cape Flattery, either."

"Nothing's going to happen to me, Hannah.

106

I wasn't mean to Howard when he was alive."
I turned around and opened the front door
without saying anything else.

I slipped quietly into our living room. Hannah followed me. I didn't try to stop her.

"What happened, Billy? Tell me!" It was
Mom. She had startled us both and had sent
my heart racing.

I looked around the darkened room. When
my eyes finally adjusted, I could see her sitting
on the sofa. "Could I turn on a light first?" It
scared me to see her so frightened like this,
but then, after what Mrs. Winter had just told
me, maybe I should have been more frightened, too.

I turned on the overhead light before I re-
ceived a reply.

"What's she doing here?" Mom demanded.
She stood up.

"She wants to help us, Mom." I wasn't quite
sure how sincere Hannah was, but I didn't
know what else to say. I started toward the
kitchen. "I'm hungry. I'm going to fix Hannah
and me something to eat."

Mom and Hannah followed me.

"Some people came around here," Mom said.
"They were looking for Howard."

I took a jar of mayonnaise out of the refrigerator and started spreading it on some bread. "They didn't find him, did they?"

"No, but they didn't want to leave," Mom said. "They blame Howard for all of this, Billy. They blame you, too."

"It's not Howard's fault," I said. "He didn't want to die." I was trying to stay calm, but it wasn't easy. "They can't blame him for what's happening. They can't blame me, either."

I had finished making the sandwiches. "Come on, Hannah. Let's go to my room."

Mom stayed in the kitchen.

Hannah and I ate the sandwiches in silence.

When we finished, I looked at my watch. "It's only about an hour until dark."

Hannah nodded.

"Tell me what to do, Hannah. I can't figure it out."

"There's nothing to figure out, Billy. It will happen, whether you want it to or not. It has already been decided. The only thing you can do is get out of Cape Flattery."

Deep down, I knew she was right. What could I really do to stop all of this? "The police have set up road blocks, though. We'd never make it past those."

Hannah took a set of keys out of her coat pocket and handed them to me. "They won't stop you if you're in one of our church vans. They'll think you're members."

"We'll take you with us, Hannah."

"That's what I really wanted, Billy, when I ran after you, but now I know I can't. I have to go back and try to get my mother to see that letting Chief Rury take over the church is all wrong." She sighed. "I just wanted to make sure you were . . . all right."

We sat in the silence of my room, allowing the darkness to envelop us.

"How can we get the . . ." I started to say, but Mom's screams from the kitchen stopped me.

I turned and bolted from the room.

From the hallway, I could hear horrible growling sounds. They were the same sounds that Howard had made when he had tried to attack Mr. Calhoun. "Oh, please, no," I murmured.

When I reached the door to the kitchen, I could see Mom collapsed on the floor. She looked like she had fallen out of her chair. She wasn't moving.

Howard was standing in the middle of the room.

"Howard!" I screamed.

He turned and grinned at me.

"Don't touch her, Howard!"

I was sure he had understood me, but it obviously didn't matter, for he lunged at Mom's arm.

I grabbed him by the neck and began pulling, but Howard wouldn't let go. In fact, I was sure his strength was several times what it had been when he was alive.

Still, I continued to tug at him. "Help me!" I shouted.

Hannah was standing at the kitchen door now.

"Help me, Hannah!"

She didn't move.

I turned back and pulled again at Howard's throat with all my might.

He let go of Mom's arm and, with a ferocious growl, pushed me clear across the room. I landed with a thud. Sharp pains shot through my side.

I couldn't move. I lay there with my eyes closed.

I had rented this horror movie, I was thinking, one that I really didn't want to watch again, but the man at the video store had told me I had to, and that was that.

What I actually wanted to do was to close my eyes and go to sleep, but there was a new law in Cape Flattery that said you had to

110

watch the same movie every night before you could close your eyes.

Then I heard stirring sounds. I opened my eyes. Mom was waking up, I realized. I managed to turn over.

"Let me help you, Mrs. Baker," Hannah said. Relief rushed over me. I realized she was still alive.

Howard was nowhere around. How had he gotten in and out? I wondered. I could see that the back door to the kitchen was closed. Could resurrected pets open and close doors? Then I saw the open window and realized that Howard had come in that way. That was a relief. At least they couldn't just walk through solid walls.

Outside, I was sure I could hear more screams.

I pulled myself up. Some way, I had to get to Dr. Holmes's clinic and let him know about the church van.

I told Hannah what I was planning to do. I asked her if she could at least come with me, in case Dr. Holmes had any questions about how to get the van without any of the church members knowing about it.

"I guess I can do that," she said.

I was also hoping that maybe I could still talk her into going with us.

Hannah looked at Mom, who was now lying on the bed in her room. "What are you going to do about her?"

"She'll just have to stay here by herself until we're ready to leave Cape Flattery." I looked around. "We'll make sure all the doors and windows are locked."

I walked out the front door and almost collided with Howard. "You!" I cried. The built up anger exploded out of me and I forgot all about Dr. Holmes. I flung myself at him.

But Howard moved out of the way, and I landed with a huge thud on the wooden porch. I was sure that I had cracked a rib in the fall.

Howard growled.

I moved my head where I could see him. "Come on, you coward!" I shouted. "Let's see you try to attack me!"

Howard just looked at me.

"Well, what are you waiting for?" I shouted.

"Billy!" Hannah was watching me from the front door, a look of terror in her eyes.

"Stay away, Hannah. This isn't your problem. If he's going to attack me, he's just going to attack me!"

113

"He's not, though, Billy," Hannah said. She stepped out onto the front porch.

Howard growled again. It was just a low rumbling sound, but it was terrifying all the same. Still, he remained standing where he was. The smell of death hung around him, and it was all I could do to keep from throwing up.

"What does he want, then?" I asked.

"I think he . . . he wants to say he's sorry," Hannah replied.

Through opaque eyes, I could see Howard looking at me. For a minute I was sure I could really see the old Howard, the pet I had raised from a small puppy, looking at me, pleading for forgiveness.

"Is it over, Howard?" I held my breath. Maybe, just maybe, Mrs. Winter was wrong!

"Look!" Hannah cried. "He's nodding his head."

I wasn't sure, but yes, there had been some movement there. Was Howard really answering my question?

"Is it *really* . . ." I started to ask again.

But Howard turned and walked slowly down the porch steps.

He stopped when he reached the sidewalk, but after hesitating for just a few seconds, he continued down the street.

"We have to follow him and see where he's going," I said.

Hannah helped me up.

"Be careful!" I cried. "I think I cracked a rib."

Finally I was on my feet, and together, we started down the steps.

When we reached the sidewalk, we could see Howard standing under a street lamp. We stopped and watched him for a moment. He raised his head and let out a bloodcurdling howl.

"What's he doing?" I asked.

"I think he's sending some kind of message to the other resurrected pets," Hannah replied. "Maybe he's calling them all to go back with him, so they can rebury themselves!"

"I just hope that's it," I said.

It had occurred to me that Howard could have lured us away from the house so that we could be attacked.

Animals suddenly began appearing from the darkness of the bushes and trees around us, but fortunately they didn't act at all interested in us. They immediately got in step behind Howard.

"That can only mean one thing, Hannah."

"What?"

"They just wanted to scare people—maybe to warn them to treat animals better."

"If that's true, Billy, then you may not have to leave Cape Flattery after all," Hannah said excitedly.

"That's right!"

We had followed the resurrected pets for several blocks before I finally realized where we were.

"Look, Hannah!" I pointed up ahead. "Dr. Holmes's clinic! I hadn't realized we turned onto the street that went past it."

"It looks deserted to me," Hannah said.

It looked deserted to me, too, but I was just hoping that Dr. Holmes was somewhere inside.

When we finally reached it, we slowed down, but the pack of resurrected pets following Howard continued on without stopping.

"He has to be here," I said. "He may have heard the animals coming and turned off the lights."

We stood in the street until the end of the pack was about a half a block away.

Then we ran to the clinic, and I knocked on the front door. "Dr. Holmes?"

There was no sound from inside.

I tried the door. It opened.

"Dr. Holmes! It's Billy!"

At the end of the hallway, a door opened

slowly, letting out a dim light, and Dr. Holmes appeared in the door. "What do you want, Billy?" he called. I could see that his right arm was bandaged.

"I think it's over," I called to him. I started walking slowly toward him.

As I did, Dr. Holmes's other hand came out slowly from behind his back. He was holding a revolver.

I stopped. "It really is over," I repeated. My voice broke, so I cleared my throat to cover it. I couldn't start losing it now.

Dr. Holmes wasn't quite aiming the revolver at me, but one false move on my part, and he'd probably shoot me. For all he knew, given the way people were thinking in Cape Flattery, he could have decided that I had been in on all of this from the start.

"They're on their way back to the cemetery now," Hannah said. "They just wanted to send people a message about treating animals better, that's all."

For a minute, I had even forgotten she was there. Her speaking seemed to break the spell in the room.

Dr. Holmes dropped the hand holding the gun. "How do you know that's what they're doing?"

I told him everything that had happened in the last few minutes, then I added, "I don't think we'll have to leave Cape Flattery after all." Seeing his arm up close stopped me. There were several deep gashes in it. "What happened?"

Dr. Holmes sat down on the floor and leaned up against the wall. "Howard. He came here tonight and attacked me."

I had known all along that Howard might try to do that, but it still came as a shock to me. "I'm sorry." That sounded stupid, I knew, but I didn't know what else to say. "Well, it's all over now, though. It really is."

"I don't believe it, Billy. I'll never believe it. They'll be back. Mark my word. Maybe not tomorrow night or the night after that, but they'll be back. I saw it in Howard's eyes."

Even after all that had happened, my first reaction was to take Howard's side, but I decided not to say anything.

"Somehow we have to make sure that never happens," Dr. Holmes continued. He thought for a minute. "They should never have put that pet cemetery there in the first place. They should have stuck to the original plan."

I looked up at him. "What was the original plan?"

118

"They were going to build a parking lot for the human cemetery. If they had done it, then that whole place would now be covered with concrete!"

I blinked. "That's it!" I cried.

"What?" Hannah and Dr. Holmes asked in unison.

I was really getting excited now. "The pets in the pet cemetery were all just wrapped in shrouds and then buried. It was easy for them to come back, because all they had to do was bite or claw their way out of the shroud and then dig their way up through the ground."

"I don't understand what you're getting at," Dr. Holmes said.

"You gave me the answer to this yourself. Once the resurrected animals are back in their graves, we can cover the whole cemetery with concrete. They'll be sealed in and won't ever be able to get out again."

Dr. Holmes didn't say anything, but I could tell he was thinking about it.

"What makes you think it'll work, Billy?" Hannah asked.

"Well, people have to let the resurrected pets get into their houses. Since we know they can't just come through wooden doors or brick walls, they certainly won't be able to dig themselves out of concrete!"

Dr. Holmes stood up. "My Jeep's in back, but first I need to call Bob Cannon on my CB. He's a contractor and lays all the concrete foundations for buildings here in town!"

II

Hannah got into the front seat of the Jeep with Dr. Holmes. I sat in the back.

"What I want to do is make sure the resurrected pets are actually going to the cemetery," Dr. Holmes said. "Bob Cannon's getting his men ready to roll right now. All I have to do is give him the signal."

We finally found the pets five blocks away.

"There they are," I whispered. I wasn't sure why I had whispered, because we were inside the Jeep. Maybe I was just afraid that the attacks would start all over again, if the pets got wind of what we were planning to do.

We didn't get that close to them, though.

"Well, it certainly looks like that's where they're headed all right," Dr. Holmes said.

I was absolutely amazed at how many resurrected pets were in the streets ahead of us, and more and more of them were still coming from the side streets and out of people's front yards.

"We'll whip around the block here and get ahead of them," Dr. Holmes said.

"Do you think they can get the pet cemetery paved over by tomorrow night?" I asked him.

"I hope so. They're planning to pave over at least fifty yards on each side of it. Those pets won't be able to get out again in this century!"

Dr. Holmes got on the car radio and talked to several people, giving all kinds of complicated directions, but when he finished, he reattached the speaker to his CB and said, "They're rolling!"

We were on Mansfield Street now, which paralleled the street that all the pets were on, and in a few minutes we came to Juniper Road, which would take us to the road that went to the cemetery.

Before we could turn onto it, though, we had to wait for several large trucks to pass. They had CAPE FLATTERY CONSTRUCTION COMPANY written on their sides.

"There goes the parking lot," Dr. Holmes said, as he pulled in behind the last truck.

When we finally reached the main entrance, Dr. Holmes followed the cement trucks as they pulled out onto a grassy area that bordered the pet cemetery and headed toward the rear. A road grader was already parked there.

Dr. Holmes parked the Jeep next to one of the cement trucks and got out.

Hannah and I followed.

"How long will it take to get this place covered up?" Dr. Holmes asked one of the cement truck drivers.

"We'll need most of the day, but it'll be done before they think about coming back out," the man said. He looked over at me. "Your dog started all of this, didn't he?"

I returned the man's look. "No, sir. Our neighbor, Mr. Calhoun, started it all." I didn't wait for the man to respond but turned and walked around to the other side of the Jeep.

Hannah followed.

"It's always going to be like that," I said. "This will always be my fault, because Howard was my dog. It's going to get worse, too, when people start talking to each other. They'll probably try to lynch me."

Hannah didn't say anything.

In the distance, I could hear a rumbling noise and muted whining and grunting. "They're coming," I whispered to Hannah. "They're coming."

Dr. Holmes came around to where we were

standing. "As soon as the last pet has reburied itself, they'll bulldoze down the tombstones and then the men will start pouring the concrete."

From where we were standing—with the help of the moon—it was possible to see across the cemetery to the entrance, as the first wave of resurrected pets began arriving. They were making horrible grunting and whining sounds and were moving very slowly. I looked at my watch. It was four o'clock in the morning, but I wasn't a bit sleepy.

Dr. Holmes had now joined Mr. Cannon, who was directing his cement truck driver to begin circling the perimeters of the cemetery.

Some of the animals were now at the rear of the cemetery and had started to rebury themselves. It made a strange spectacle to see them crawling back down into the cracks in the graves and then trying to cover themselves up.

The reburial seemed to go on forever, although I could tell by my watch that it had only taken about two hours.

Finally, just as the first shades of pink appeared on the eastern horizon, it was all quiet.

"I think we can start bulldozing down the tombstones now," Mr. Cannon said.

For just a minute, Dr. Holmes didn't say anything. Then he looked at Mr. Cannon. "Let's check all of the graves first."

"What for?" Mr. Cannon said.

Dr. Holmes didn't answer but headed straight for Howard's grave.

I waited for a minute before I followed.

Dr. Holmes reached Howard's grave, looked down, then started waving his hands wildly. "I need a flashlight! Somebody bring a flashlight over here!"

I stopped dead still.

Mr. Cannon rushed past me and handed Dr. Holmes a flashlight.

I felt myself going all cold inside. "What's wrong?" I called.

"He's not here!" Dr. Holmes cried.

"Whose grave is this?" Mr. Cannon demanded.

I swallowed hard. "Howard's," I whispered.

12

The pet cemetery in Cape Flattery was finally paved over, but not until three days later, after the entire town and the surrounding area had been searched for any signs of Howard. He wasn't found, and about two hundred armed citizens, who had been keeping a vigil at the cemetery, demanded that it be covered with the concrete parking lot.

By that time, Hannah and her mother had already left Cape Flattery. Although Chief Rury tried to talk the rest of the members of the Church of the Kingdom of Resurrected Pets into staying and naming him their new spiritual leader, they all left town, too. Chief Rury followed soon afterward. This was before the citizens of Cape Flattery set fire to the church building.

Dr. Holmes hid me and Mom in a small attic

room at his clinic. Several times angry mobs came there looking for us. One time I peeked through a tiny crack in the floor and saw Danny Crawford standing below me. I was sort of disappointed.

No one ever found us, though.

Dr. Holmes said that most people in Cape Flattery finally decided that Howard had gotten into the wrong grave and had probably been reburied anyway. He was sure that just made them feel better, because now that they had had their revenge, they wanted to forget everything that had happened.

He said he didn't know what to believe anymore.

One night, about two weeks after all of this had happened, Dr. Holmes packed a few things, hid me and Mom in his Jeep, and we drove out of Cape Flattery for good.

We were headed for a town in a state on the other side of the country. Dr. Holmes didn't tell us the name of the town until we were almost there.

I didn't close my eyes until we had crossed the California state line into Nevada, and then I only slept in fits until we reached Utah. We only stopped for food, gas, and to use the restroom.

Finally, when we crossed into Colorado, I began to relax.

Early one morning, we stopped for breakfast in Glenwood Springs. After we finished eating, Mom and Dr. Holmes were lingering over their coffee. I had the feeling they wanted to talk, so I told them I was going to walk around outside to get some fresh air.

The restaurant was set in a beautiful wooded area. I walked around the building twice. Just as I started around it for a third time, I noticed some movement behind one of the trees. Cold chills raced up and down my spine, and the hair at the back of my neck literally stood up.

I walked slowly toward the edge of the trees.

When I was just a few yards from it, I stopped.

Howard had appeared from behind a tree.

"You!" I cried.

He opened his mouth. His teeth were blood-red. I didn't even want to think about how that had happened.

Then he disappeared.

I stood there, unmoving.

Suddenly, a hand touched my shoulder, and I almost jumped out of my skin.

"Are you all right?" Mom asked.

I took a deep breath. "Yes," I said. "I'm all right."

Of course, I really wasn't.

We've lived in Portland, Maine, for almost two years now. Mom and Dr. Holmes got married the day we arrived.

I've never told anyone what I saw at that restaurant in Glenwood Springs, Colorado, but I wake up several times every night, thinking I'm hearing Howard scratching on my bedroom window.

I know one of these mornings it really will be him, and then the nightmare will start all over again, except this time it will be much worse.

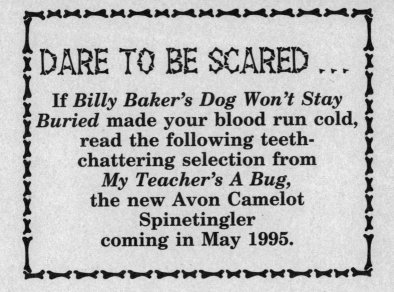

DARE TO BE SCARED ...

If *Billy Baker's Dog Won't Stay Buried* made your blood run cold, read the following teeth-chattering selection from *My Teacher's A Bug,* the new Avon Camelot Spinetingler coming in May 1995.

I didn't have time to gasp or think about it because the downstairs bell rang, and there, at the door, was my teacher the bug with another bug who looked exactly like him, except Mr. Mantis introduced it as his wife, "Trudy."

Trudy? Couldn't these imposter bugs come up with more real-sounding names?

"Trudy, hi," said Mom. Fortunately Trudy Mantis was holding a bowl in her hands, otherwise Mom would have gotten a handful of insect paw.

"Hello, Ryan," said Mr. Mantis, looking across the room at me.

I just stared at him. "You have got to be kidding."

Mom gave me an even worse look, then smiled at this hideous insect couple. "Come on inside, please. It's so nice to finally have some

133

company. We know so few people here in town. Just a few from my husband's job and well . . ."

"I'm out at the base," said Dad.

"And can't talk about your job." Mr. Mantis nodded. "I understand completely."

As they came into the living room, Mrs. Mantis handed Mom the bowl she was carrying. "A side dish to go with dinner," she said.

"Oh." Mom smiled, pulling off the lid to look inside. Forget about the thought of being eaten alive by wasp larvas—this was the moment I almost passed out.

Seeing the contents of that bowl was worse than being stung—maybe because it felt like my brain was being stung. The bowl was full of bug food! Mantis food.

Other smaller, deader bugs.

"It's sort of an old family recipe," said Mrs. Mantis, following Mom into the kitchen.

"Mmmm," said Mom. "It certainly smells delicious."

"Yeah, I'll try it," shouted Anthony from the stairs; he was on his way back down. "Of course I'll try anything."

"So what do you do, Trudy? Are you a teacher, too?" Mom was asking all the normal questions.

"Oh, no," said my teacher's bug-wife. "I just sort of hang around the house."

"Killing flies?" I asked.

"Excuse me?" said the startled Mrs. Mantis.

"Ignore him," said Mom. "He thinks he's being funny."

Dad murmured to me, "Watch it, guy. This is one of your teachers, after all."

"I told you what he was," I answered.

"Behave."

"This dish smells so unusual," Mom said. "I can't wait to taste it. What did you say it was made from?"

I almost gagged. What was Mom saying? Why couldn't she see this stuff for what it was? Pheromones.

I shook my head to clear the image, but it remained—there was no denying what Mom was about to serve for dinner, whether she meant to or not.

I followed them into the dining room to get a better look; Mom placed the bowl on the set table. As always, Anthony was rude, pouring himself a glass of tea without waiting, but that wasn't important. What was important was this: The huge glass serving dish was full of sautéed flies. Millions of them in a gravy, and Mom was about to stick a big spoon in and taste it. . . .

"Ahhhh!" Without even planning ahead I let

out a shriek, grabbed the tablecloth with all of the strength I could muster, and pulled. The balance of the table was offset, and everything careened to the left with a huge crash as everyone jumped out of the way. Roast beef, potatoes, cranberry sauce and sautéed house-flies crashed down together, completely un-eatable now, and I scrammed, running up the stairs.

The knock on the door took all of a minute. It was Dad; he was pale and almost in a stut-tering rage. "Have you . . . lost your mind?"

"No, Dad, I . . ."

"Your mother is down there near tears. You just humiliated this entire family? Do you real-ize that?"

"Something really bad is happening, Dad."

"I just saw something really bad happen."

"No, I mean really bad. What's going on at the base, Dad? What are you doing out there?"

"Ryan, you know I can't talk about any of that. And don't change the subject."

"That is the subject. Do you know anybody named Van Gelder?"

"What?"

"Terri Van Gelder. She was crying today, re-ally crying, and she says her dad works at the base with you and—"

"I'm not getting into that right now, Ryan. Good God, what has gotten into you?"

"Can I have a minute?"

It was a new voice in the hall, and Dad and I looked up at the same time.

In the doorway was Mr. Mantis, and even with my now-spinning brain there was no doubt about it. He was a bug, a six foot tall, twitching insect with antennas and a gaping maw, and he said, "Phil, let me talk to the boy a minute alone . . ."

"No," I started to say, "I don't want to." But I couldn't choke the words above a whisper because this bug-monster was in my room now, his shadow falling across me, and I felt like cowering under the bed.

Then Dad said the most terrible words in the history of all mankind: "Sure, maybe that'll help; I'll be downstairs. . . ."